The Living Herbalist

Jill Davies and her partner practise Natural Herbal Healing at Thornham Herb Garden, Thornham Magna, Suffolk. She qualified in horticulture at the Royal Botanical Gardens, Kew and at the RHS, Wisley, and is a Master Herbalist with the School of Natural Healing of Utah, USA — she is now co-director of the school's UK facility. She is a member of the British Herbal Medicine Association and of the Council for the British Herb Trade Association.

Apart from her work in Natural Healing she is well-known for her development of many exciting and original tea blends to be drunk for pleasure and for health. She teaches and broadcasts on the subject of herbalism, including lecturing for Cambridge University.

Some of the information offered in this book is for interest and educational purposes only. Persons who believe they are suffering from serious illness should consult a practitioner and then work with them and the book if desired.

Elderflower

flower
actual size

JILL DAVIES

The Living Herbalist

FIRST STEPS TOWARDS
NATURAL HEALING

Foreword by Kenneth Robinson,
General Secretary of the British
Herbal Medicine Association

Elm Tree Books
LONDON

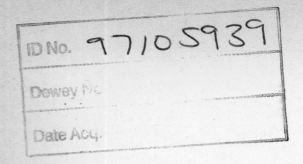

First published in Great Britain 1985
by Elm Tree Books/Hamish Hamilton Ltd
Garden House 57-59 Long Acre London WC2E 9JZ

Copyright © 1985 by Jill Davies

Herb drawings by Stephen Sturgess
Other drawings by Beryl Sanders

British Library Cataloguing in Publication Data

Davies, Jill, *1955-*
 The living herbalist: first steps toward
 natural healing.
 1. Herbs   2. Nutrition
 I. Title
 613.2'8   TX558.H4
 ISBN 0-241-11412-8

Filmset by Pioneer
Printed and bound in Great Britain by
Richard Clay (The Chaucer Press) Ltd, Bungay, Suffolk

This book is dedicated to my teachers who have given myself and many others inspiration for life: Trude Roberts, The School of Natural Healing, Dr J. R. Christopher and Dr Sharm Singha

Contents

Acknowledgements

I have to thank many people for help with this book and the dedication shows who deserves a large share of that thanks.

However, also a very warm thank you to Kitty Campion for her consistent help, sound advice and loyal friendship.

Nick, a special thank you for your ready ear and 'sounding-board' abilities; also to the rest of the family for all their domestic help which made much of the time for this book possible.

Many thanks to the patients who contributed in writing towards this book but also to all those who didn't, to all telephone callers, letter writers, and visitors.

Stephen Sturgess and Beryl Sanders: thank you both for your beautiful illustrations for the book, Stephen for the exquisite plant drawings and Beryl for the rest.

Thank you all at the Natural Therapeutic Centre, Gislingham, for your loving support and warmth.

A very large thank you must go to Sue Strickland not just for being an excellent typist and a very necessary and good speller, but for having the special ability on being able to arrange sensibly notes squeezed in on already untidy long-hand.

Thank you the British Herbal Medicine Association for your constant support, and especially Mr Kenneth Robinson, the association's secretary.

Finally thanks to Gloria Ferris for being such a supportive agent and to Elm Tree Books, especially Caroline Taggart, for making this book a reality.

Foreword

Plant medicine is basic and 'natural'; its roots lie deep in a historical tradition. More than any other kind of medicine it can claim to have been tested by time.

The herbalist knows what this means, and for practitioners like Jill Davies, the author of this book, such knowledge has been refined and enriched by their own experience and that of their patients. But it is not enough to be satisfied with what you are doing: there is need to analyse and explain to others the principles on which you work, so that they can first assess, and then perhaps sample, the contribution made by Herbal Medicine to good health.

As Secretary of the British Herbal Medicine Association I receive an increasing number of requests for such information. They come from a wide variety of people — from children engaged on school projects, students at Universities and Polytechnics, nurses, social workers, pharmacists, local authorities, and large numbers of individuals who, for different reasons, ranging from dissatisfaction with existing treatments to a simple and healthy curiosity about alternative methods, turn to us with their questions.

This is just one reason for welcoming this new book from one of our members, because it will help me in performing one of the declared objects of our Association which is 'to encourage the diffusion of knowledge about herbal remedies'. But this is also a good book in its own right, well written, competent and eminently readable.

One thing above all stands out in Jill Davies' presentation of the Herbal Alternative — she demonstrates abundantly that Herbalism is quite remote from that concept of medicine which has as its basic aim the instantaneous cure of specific ailments. More properly it is concerned with a whole way of life in which the right foods combine with herbs and herbal remedies to assist the body naturally to perform its proper function in countering illness and fostering good health. Not everyone will agree with all the articles of Jill Davies' faith, but few who read this book with an open mind will fail to be impressed by the sincerity and conviction of the author and come away with a much clearer picture of what Herbalism is about.

What is more, no honest reader will escape without finding something here which will enable him or her to modify and improve their existing style of life. For *The Living Herbalist* is not just a description of the principles of Herbalism: it challenges the reader to take responsibility for his or her own health and happiness and outlines a variety of positive steps to achieve this end.

Kenneth Robinson

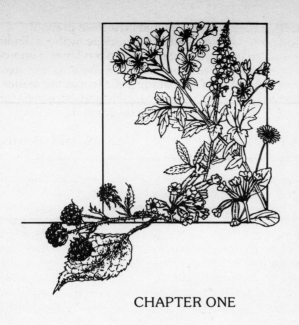

CHAPTER ONE

Introduction

THE LIVING HERBALIST DEFINED

This is not a 'home herbal' or quick healing guide, with advice about which plant or plants are to be used for specific problems, nor is it a dictionary of botanical descriptions. There are many excellent books on these topics which will be a natural progression from this one. This book aims to introduce you to the theories and practice of natural healing in a very simple way. It was written to fill the need of people saying, 'Please start at the beginning, I'm confused'. It is a philosophy of herbalism, with healing methods being discussed as part of the broader subject. It will help you to be better informed and more selective if you are seeking treatment or using safe, simple self-help methods. It aims to make you stop and think before plunging in and making mistakes due to insufficient understanding; and it seeks to explain and give confidence to the scathing, doubting or frightened. It also aims to encourage you to use all forms of natural healing and not to treat them as a last resort, which makes the job of natural healing twice as difficult.

The book seeks to revive forgotten instincts; it aims to promote

1

the use of plants as food and drink, forming part of everyday life in an exciting, stimulating and enjoyable fashion. Plants are to be used to balance the system in preventive terms as well as restoring peak health or ridding the body of chronic illness. Whatever your reasons for being interested in living herbalism, you can gain in physical, mental or spiritual terms.

The Different Attitudes required for Preventive Medicine

In order to practise preventive medicine, you have to consider the whole body, and also take into account psychological and external factors. Conventional or 'allopathic' medicine is now beginning to consider preventive treatment, but its whole approach is based on curing or preventing a specific, isolated ailment in the short term. Herbal medicine does not simply tell you to give up cigarettes or cut down on cholesterol. What herbal medicine gives is health and a long-term lifestyle awareness, all in one package. Its slow and thorough healing process gives rise to an understanding of how sickness originates in the patient's mind and body, and its results are permanent.

The principal difference between allopathic and natural medicine is that allopathic medicine aims to suppress symptoms with drugs, rather than help the body to use its own healing mechanisms to eliminate the toxins that caused the disease. Natural medicine and its use of herbs strive to support, balance and gently persuade the body to do the healing for itself, so that next time it will actually perform its own repair functions. What stops a body from healing itself is the bad diet and living habits to which we are educated from birth and which mean that the body is never healthy enough to deal with itself properly. Psychological factors may also contribute.

The other major difference between the two forms of medicine is that conventional treatment can appear to work miracles, producing instant cures, however temporarily. Natural healing requires more time and effort on the part of the patient — but the long-term results are well worth it! Nonetheless natural methods frequently work considerably faster in healing time than many conventional treatments and can be a better option for this reason alone.

It is not easy for people to give up the treatment they have been programmed since birth to accept silently and surrenderingly, and instead respond to their own instincts and body language. Fear and allied emotions can block the healing process, and it is hard for some people to accept that a parochial-sounding remedy like lavender cream can be a better cure for acne and eczema than the

2

steroid cream their GP prescribed. As my teacher Dr Christopher* used to say, 'There are no incurable diseases, but at times there are incurable patients!' Mystified when I first heard these words, I have now had his statement proved to me time and time again. The herbs will get on and do their job quite happily, but only if the mind of the patient will let them.

So many of the concepts of natural healing methods and the use of preventive medicine are foreign to our society. That is why there is a tremendous need for enlightenment, so that people are encouraged to adopt the philosophy into their daily lives. We will start at the beginning and try to build up a fundamental understanding of the whole subject. There will be a lot of undoing to be done, but even if you reach an awkward grasp of living herbalism, perhaps your children will grow up to find it normal and natural.

What do we do wrong?

There are four categories which conspire towards ill-health: psychological, ecological, physiological and biological factors.

Much of today's illness is simply due to wrong diet. The body produces warning signals in the form of acute illness, like constant colds, glandular swellings, poor circulation, etc. Conventionally, this illness is treated without considering its root cause — and so at some point the symptoms recur, resulting in a chronic illness, which is much more difficult to treat. Treating the disease when it is at its acute stage — 'catching it early' — is much easier. This often means bringing the crisis to a head, using herbs to make sure the body is fully rid of its toxins. If not, the toxins may well come flooding back, and although the illness may subside for a while it will recur again and again, until perhaps the ailment becomes so bad that it is 'chronic', or general ill-health and debilitation push the body into a chronically ill condition. Treating acute ailments with 'wonder drugs' merely pushes back the problems so that they recur later, paving the way for chronic illness, perhaps of a seemingly unrelated nature. A recognisable chain might be persistent chills, flu and colds finally resulting in pneumonia: a less obvious one might be constipation as a child and arthritis as an adult.

Processed, artificially coloured, 'dead' foods are produced in vast quantities and marketed by wealthy and powerful companies. (I will talk more about 'dead' and 'alive' foods — sprouted seeds, low-

* Dr J. R. Christopher started the 'School of Natural Healing' in Utah, USA, over fifty years ago. He is dead now, but he was hailed as America's top 'whole-istic' herbalist. Having trained under his philosophies, I remain deeply indebted to his wisdom.

3

cooked grains, etc — in Chapter 3.) Millions of pounds are spent on advertising 'junk' and 'convenience' food, while not even comparable thousands are spent on nutritional education. I see so many patients who live on frozen vegetables, packet soups and instant puddings. And this is not always because the chief cook/shopper is also working full time, but because they have been seduced by advertising and think these foods are convenient. But preparing good, wholesome food does not mean you have to resort to spending hours in the kitchen. It merely requires a true understanding of food values. Many of the meals I produce for the family each night take no longer than twenty minutes to prepare and cook (often the time that 'instant' foods take anyway), but they are wholesome, alive and interesting, and I have enjoyed the time spent in producing them. If I'm tired or feeling disinclined to cook, then someone else takes over or it's muesli and fruit! Never cook if you're feeling angry or ill — a junk food meal prepared with love and warmth is better than the best wholefood meal cooked with aggression and resentment.

Western malnutrition is a good description of what a large number of people are suffering from in this country today. Children very often come off worst, becoming overweight and lacking in energy, and suffering anything from sinus problems to bad temper, laziness and aggression, their lifestyle and food intake all conspiring against them. Because so many people lack any real understanding of food values, they do not suspect that some of their diet is dangerous, and that the food they eat may be almost totally lacking in vitamins and minerals, which in turn means that the body is less able to assimilate food properly or deal with viruses, infections etc. Excessive fat intake comes not only from butter, fried foods and chocolate but also from meat and milk, while five-sixths of most people's sugar intake is not in the obvious packet form but occurs in soft drinks, sweets, cakes, even such processed sauces as tomato ketchup. Even overcooked and stodgy school dinners are often better than the 'nourishment' children get at home, and we are breeding a new generation of very sick people mentally, physically and emotionally, with critically low levels of iron and calcium. In America they are beginning to turn the tide with their children, starting to teach nutrition in schools and revising school menus. Let's hope we can do the same.

Addiction

Amid all the publicity about drug abuse and glue-sniffing we are rarely told about the addictive qualities of many common foods. Few people are aware how much they depend on sugar and salt for an instant 'buzz' at times of depression. This is one of the reasons why it is so hard to give up chocolate or crisps, even though we do realise vaguely that they are 'bad for us'. We are given sweets as appeasers at a very early age and most of us are totally hooked by the time we are two years old!

What can we do about it?

The new craze for health and fitness is one that is here to stay, with more and more people taking an interest in exercise and diet (yet the majority of patients I have seen have never been into a health-food or a wholefood shop in their lives). A lot of manufacturers and advertisers are latching on to this new awareness, exploiting the fact that much of the public is only partially educated about 'good food'.

Brown bread has come to be known as 'good for you', but colour alone does not mean anything: certain bread companies merely dye their white bread to lure the health-conscious. 'Wholemeal' is the word to look for, and this coupled with 'organic' and 'stone ground' describe the best bread possible.

Another craze is for muesli, but again so many brands have vast quantities of sugar added to appeal to our badly trained taste-buds. You may be eating muesli thinking how much good it is doing you, but is it really? It's much better to mix your own from natural ingredients: then you can be sure that only the best has gone into it.

Another fad is for decaffeinated coffee. Many people have come to recognise some of the harms of coffee, even though television, films and advertisements are full of people drinking it. However, decaffeination only removes the caffeine and leaves behind the harmful acids, perhaps even more harmful in their unstable state. Another point that is often missed is that tea contains two and a half times as much caffeine as coffee.

But these are isolated examples. Becoming a 'living herbalist' means a daily commitment to searching out foods that are alive, and enjoying the whole experience (yet without the confines of being over-obsessed or 'unbalanced'), even when eating in a restaurant or snack bar. Herbs and food are your daily weapon against ill health. You can diminish the chances of sickness and make the need to use more intensive natural and herbal healing less likely. Searching out good foods can be a difficult process because some of us are naturally aware of the dangers of supermarket food but let our guard fall when walking into a wholefood or healthfood shop. You have to become a dedicated label-reader — and make sure you are not fooled by the often more expensive so-called 'healthfoods'. Only pressure from well-informed customers will force these out of the shops.

Don't make the mistake of believing that healthy food is too expensive to eat all the time. Actually I know I spend a lot less than most people on my weekly shopping bill, and we all feel we eat very well and enjoyably. There is so much unemployment nowadays I often hear people worrying about how little they have to spend on food, but they are trying to spend it on tins and packets in supermarkets! And as so many people now have so much spare time, what could be better than an increase in the current swing back to allotments for growing vegetables? It provides self-employment, cheaper, fresher food and exercise all in one.

What part do herbs play in daily diet?

I rarely separate 'herbs' from 'food' in my own mind, but I am continually reminded that most people do. The same applies to spices which are frequently used in healing but which are seldom considered part of our diets. A vegetable gelatine capsule containing nothing but ginger and cayenne pepper may often be recommended as an addition to daily diet as part of a healing programme. Likewise spices will be encouraged as part of our daily menu.

Think of the way old cookery books combine all sorts of natural ingredients in their recipes. Is it any wonder that people suffer from constipation, indigestion, flatulence and headaches after meals when so many of us have forgotten the food combinations our ancestors used to promote digestion and absorption? These people were natural and instinctive living herbalists!

What do herbs do?

Herbs work on many different levels and they are potent and effective in the body.

There are tonic herbs to feed the entire system, making assimilation of other herbs and plants easier. They provide all our necessary vitamins and minerals in a natural, organic and assimilable form. Herbs can correct energy and blood circulation, deflecting morbid accumulation and congestion and helping digestion and elimination. They can remove excess water in the body, clear fevers by lowering temperature and detoxify, stimulate and build fevers to provide safe elimination of toxins. Some induce perspiration and vomiting when necessary, while others neutralise and stabilise. They exert their complex structures on toning, building and strengthening all organs and systems, and their healing powers are long-term. They can be used for major or minor ailments, emergency treatment or long-standing illnesses, acute or chronic conditions.

6

Which form of treatment should I go for?

The simple answer to this question is that you should follow a treatment you have faith in. I'll be talking later about finding a practitioner to help you, but different cultures with all their forms of medicine understand how important it is that a patient believes in his or her treatment.

How do I know it will work?

Herbs work. They have been doing so for thousands of years and will go on doing so for many thousands more. Herbal medicine is not 'just a bit quaint', occasionally effective for minor ailments. It is a well-organised system of medical knowledge based on observation, experiment and clinical trial, all duly recorded. In China — the country with the largest population in the world — it is still the most commonly used form of medicine. A lot of the knowledge which was originally empirical has been verified by modern science. However, it must be admitted, most of the time herbalists are just happy to know that 'it works', not having the resources to analyse results and preferring to spend any spare time and money finding new knowledge.

Should I tell my GP I'm seeking an alternative to his help? Will he be hostile?

This is often a dilemma in people's minds, and quite understandably so. I always encourage people to talk over their intended treatment with their doctor; indeed, I sometimes insist if they are taking drugs he has prescribed. If the doctor is sympathetic and encouraging, this paves the way for a two-way relationship between us. However, I apply no pressure in this direction and a great deal of the time I find that patients tell their doctors when they are better, or sometimes say 'nought at all' and just relieve his busy surgery.

How do I know when to use natural or conventional treatment?

There are still occasions when I would seek conventional treatment and it may help you to know that my personal attitudes developed over many years because it does seem to be a common dilemma. I would use pain-killing injections on a child — or an adult if they wished — in the case of a road accident. I would recommend surgery to remove a foreign object such as flying glass which had

7

become lodged in the skin; for a caesarian section operation — and as this can unexpectedly become urgent, I generally recommend giving birth in hospital; or occasionally for removing or altering the function of a section of the body if life was in danger, as in an acute case of peritonitis. However, the kind of surgery that is most generally carried out is often damaging and about as logical as chopping off the head in the case of a chronic headache. I'll be talking in more detail about my attitude to the removal of tonsils or the gall-bladder, two operations very commonly and unnecessarily performed, in Chapter 4. The apparent need for this sort of surgery would be avoided if proper attention was paid to diet and preventive medicine. Certain drugs — insulin, for example — are important as their quick action can save lives, but the use of insulin would be supplanted long-term by herbs. There are other drugs and technical equipment which can save lives in an emergency, but there are also herbs which are supreme in this role and which I would probably use where conventional treatment might well be failing, for instance in the case of severe haemorrhaging. Antibiotics? These are frequently used nowadays; I would personally only use them in a 'life or death' emergency — possibly once in a lifetime.

The decision to use natural medicine in preference to conventional treatment is a hard one for most people, and again I would advise you always to do whatever you feel happy and safe doing. The ultimate responsibility rests with you; it is your body — or your child's.

Combining Conventional and Natural Treatment

This is something which a lot of people do, but some people find it hard to know how to set about it. The most important thing is to prepare the ground in advance. If for instance you are going into hospital for an operation or to have a baby, and you wish to continue to follow your natural diet, say so *before* the day you are due to go in, and make sure it is written down on your hospital records. Remember that nobody can force you to do anything you don't wish to, but by accepting the facilities and care of the hospital you have placed yourself in their hands and under their routine. Don't demand weird and wonderful menus; rely on a friend or relative to bring in what you need. And try to negotiate everything in a friendly, unemotional manner, which will achieve much more than aggressive 'battering'.

Why does natural medicine seem to fail sometimes?

The finger is so often pointed at conventional treatment failing that I feel it is only fair to explore this question with natural methods. If treatment is not successful, the blame lies either with the practitioner or with the patient. In conventional treatment it is sometimes the drugs that are to blame, but *never* can you blame a herb which fails to cure an illness. Although most herbs have specific healing powers and applications, I find that just any safe (non-toxic) herb will do something positive, however minor.

An incompetent practitioner may not use herbs to the best advantage, or he may not use a 'complete' approach, neglecting to advise on life-style, diet and the use of other therapies when necessary. In other words, he may not employ the 'whole' approach that is the basis of natural healing.

Natural healing may also fail if patients do not carry out the hard work which has to be done in order to regain health. The patients themselves may be only partially to blame here: they may not be receiving adequate family support, or may even be battling against active non-support from relatives and friends. However, many people underestimate the amount of time and self-help required to get better, having been conditioned over the years to expect quick results with no personal effort. It may also come as an unpleasant surprise to find that you have to pay a natural practitioner, but often this is used merely as an excuse to disguise a lack of conviction for the treatment. To quote one natural practitioner I know: 'You may be looking for a good doctor, but I'm looking for good patients!'

Another possible reason for failure is that the mind is not yet ready to receive treatment; I'll be talking about this more in Chapter 2.

Let me end this introduction with the story of a patient who had excellent support from his family and who worked hard at helping himself to get better. It is written by the patient's wife and may help you to understand both the commitment that natural healing requires and the rewards it brings:

David had taken doctor's pills for very high blood pressure for five months, without satisfactory results. We wanted to explore other means of treatment and consulted a herbalist. The feeling was one of absolute relief when we were told that help could be given, that there was treatment available besides just taking drugs. The remedy necessitated changes in diet, including taking herbs in tea and capsule form. The herb teas were very different from what we were used to, but we persevered and soon began to enjoy them. Drinking cayenne pepper was quite a different matter, as it gave David hiccups! He knew it would speed his recovery but it was a real strain for him.

His blood pressure was slow to respond to the herbal treatment, but after three months of really concerted effort, change of diet, weight loss, jogging and acupressure massage, he managed to lower it to normal. His doctor was confident that she didn't need to keep a check on him any more and was happy finally to leave him without his pills or check-ups. I should add here that our doctor was very co-operative during the herbal treatment and impressed by the results achieved.

The change of diet we found extremely easy to follow, mainly because we felt that it was the most sensible thing to do and made the changes gradually over a period of two to three weeks. We went through the cupboards and literally threw away anything which we knew was going to work against David's treatment. We had never been big meat eaters, and now felt we wanted to give up eating meat almost completely but were careful to plan nutritious alternatives. We stopped drinking instant coffee and now drink dandelion coffee, apple juice and herbal teas. We always use wholemeal brown bread and all baking is homemade. Our diet now consists of a home-made muesli for breakfast; we always sprout our own seeds and beans and eat many salads (and there are numerous variations), home-made soups, occasionally fish, baked potatoes, lightly steamed vegetables and fruit. We use a vegetable salt for flavouring and sugar we replaced with honey. The whole family (and this includes our three children, ages ranging from eight to sixteen) takes cayenne pepper and ginger in capsules with garlic juice daily, for our general well-being; this was our own idea.

With a bit of gentle persuasion and disguising to begin with, we have converted our children to a new diet, one we hope they will always use.

This last year has been a wonderful experience in finding out the power of herbs and what one can achieve; our children too have witnessed that herbs can cure. Our only regret is that we didn't learn of this earlier. It has given us a new outlook, enabling us to live a more complete life.

CHAPTER TWO

Lifestyle Awareness

SPIRITUAL AND PSYCHOLOGICAL ASPECTS OF HEALTH

When I was eighteen I became quite ill, although I now know that the problem had been brewing for many years. I saw a total of twelve doctors, some of them specialists, and the result was an operation and a seven-inch scar on my stomach. I left hospital after two and a half weeks having been told they didn't know what was wrong with me.

At this time I still had quite a lot of faith in doctors, and I was shattered. If they couldn't help me, who could? The answer had to lie with me. I knew nothing of natural medicine and my understanding of nutrition and diet was almost zero. I loved vegetables and fruit, but as I was a vegetarian I also consumed large quantities of milk and cheese — the ignorant vegetarian's protein substitutes! Without really knowing anything about it, I started trying to meditate and came to the conclusion that there must be some sort of self-healing technique which would use the mind and body together. This led me to Hatha yoga and my first healing teacher — a very lucky find and the best teacher of yoga I have ever met. I shall always be indebted to her (as I am to all my teachers) for the help she gave me.

A lot of my problems *were* physical, but a lot were also in my mind, and these were the hardest to come to terms with. But once I had faced up to them, I found so many doors were opened and my body's renewed health reflected a new self-awareness and self-confidence. I tell you my story because it is so similar to many other people's and because self-realisation is such a vital part of a balanced and healthy lifestyle. Few of us are born with a natural balance of mind and body. We all feel guilt or embarrassment because of our imperfections and inadequacies, but admitting that we are frightened, worried, selfish, angry or whatever is often the hardest part of all on the road to self-realisation.

The word 'balance' will keep cropping up throughout this book, whether I am talking about diet or lifestyle or healing. Balance is a vital factor in the living herbalist's philosophy, so let's start by considering the different elements which need to be correctly balanced in order to produce harmony.

Yin and Yang

According to the Chinese, in the beginning there was 'Wu-Chi', a state of 'non-differentiation'. There was no light or dark, no heat or cold, no solidity or emptiness. From this came Yang and Yin, representing respectively male and female, solidity and emptiness, light and darkness, activity and inactivity. The next evolvement is Tai Chi, a state where Yin and Yang are combined into an ever-interacting and inseparable unity. Within Yang lies the seed of Yin and within Yin lies the seed of Yang. All life is made up of these two categories and an understanding of them is an important part of a practitioner's diagnosis and can be of great assistance in a self-help treatment, for both emotional and physical imbalances. 'Allowing' the fluctuations of Yin and Yang within oneself and 'being aware of them' does much to free the spirit and unlock the mind.

Yin/Yang symbol:
Yin is water and Yang is fire; both are motivated by air, an essential factor to life

Emotional Blocks

Whenever I have to tackle this side of healing with a patient, I can just feel their defensiveness, embarrassment, shame and downright refusal to believe 'it could be in the mind'. And they have no idea how to go about changing these things. Spots and lumps can be seen, arthritis can be felt, but how can you diagnose anger or fear as the cause of your illness, much less do something about it? Often the best I can do is just to suggest finding a spiritual guide, but changing one's general lifestyle and diet can open up the doors of awareness, if it is done with true commitment.

If, after dietary and nutritional counselling, exercise suggestions, herbal treatment and other natural therapies, the patient is still not making progress, this is the time to try harder to make the person look deeper into themselves. They need to be made to find out *why* they are blocking the healing process and this often means finding the key to unlock a suppression of some kind, a past shock, present underlying unhappiness or whatever. 'Shocks' in life can mean anything from divorce or redundancy, to a major road accident or death of a loved one. Even life's natural progressions and 'high points' can provide minor 'shocks' which, if the person is in poor health can trigger all kinds of lurking problems: a new job, moving house, getting married, children leaving home or retirement, for instance. So frequently I spend time talking in general about the patient's relationships with their friends and family. I meet wives who are battling with husbands, fathers with children, neighbours with neighbours or those who would like to do those things but naturally suppress their emotions. They put up their defences, allowing feelings to fester internally instead, repressing natural emotions which they feel are ugly or might shatter their own illusions of being a 'nice' person.

I recently came across a young woman who had had a great shock as a teenager (a parent had died) but who, at the time, had shown little reaction to it. By the time she was in her thirties, it was apparently firmly buried in the past. To meet her, she was a happy, relaxed young woman and seemed to be a friendly, gregarious person. Her secret was chronic eczema on her legs and arms which she had suffered with for many years. Whenever life got 'sticky' the eczema became worse. Acupuncture, homeopathy, herbal medicine, massage, bouts of six weeks in hospital with coal tar treatments and cortizone creams were among the list of things she had tried in order to rid herself of this disease. The one thing that no one could get her to face was herself. Her hope was that the herbs, the doctor, the hospital, the diet or the creams would remove her problems, thereby allowing her to duck the responsibilities of her own illness. Interestingly enough, after months of counselling by natural healers, the final (good) blow came from the hospital when they told her not to return as there was nothing more they could do. This finally had the effect of making her realise that she must do something for herself. Facing up to the problems she'd been burying, and assuming responsibility for her own body, not only cured her eczema but improved the quality of her life and relationships generally.

The word hypochondria is a loaded one and is often used to describe any psychological illness. But real or feigned sickness needs great attention from others; impatience or lack of sympathy, a frequent reaction, is likely to make the patient worse, closing in yet harder the repressed emotions causing the illness.

My naturopathic herbalist teacher Dr Christopher cured himself of liver cancer when he was in his twenties, but it wasn't until he had discovered tremendous hate behind his kind, happy face that his road to recovery was set. His deep-seated feelings went back to the time when his mother had abandoned him to an orphanage, unable to look after him on her own. Although he was soon given a home and two loving foster parents, he bore the resentment. Facing his hate and anger, he came to understand his mother's actions, replacing his hate with love; his herbs, diet and determination all combining to heal his cancer. He lived a long and happy life, dying in his mid-eighties, having taught many people, including myself, the power of emotion to create sickness.

Certain organs are connected with certain feelings, and the Chinese have practised this association for centuries. For instance, fear is usually associated with the kidneys and genito-urinary systems. It involves the suppression of feelings and can cause sterility, cystitis, delayed menstruation or kidney disfunction. How often do we hear of a woman who is desperate to become pregnant and cannot conceive? Her worry about not becoming pregnant drives the possibility further away. Once she relaxes and gives in or indeed 'gives up' trying, she will often conceive rapidly.

Visualisation Exercises and the Placebo Effect

I recently met a lady who told me that, after hearing about the relationship of pets and humans and their emotionally stabilising effects, she had decided to try the idea out on herself. She had a cat that she loved and was determined to beat her high blood pressure using the visualisation technique. Next time she went to the doctor's to have her blood pressure taken — which is usually guaranteed to raise blood pressure still further — she simply imagined that she was stroking her cat. Her blood pressure was right down, near normal in fact . . . it had worked, and, most importantly for her, she had proof of it. Translating her new technique of visualising the love and care for her cat by stroking it, she had a ticket for life and with some dietary changes was well on the way to altering her blood pressure permanently.

Visualisation exercises can take many forms and they are useful in either inducing a state of calm or making you react in a balanced way to other people's anger or hate. In other words, they act as a defence mechanism (yet not a repression) so that other people's hang-ups and 'bad vibrations' cannot penetrate and harm you. As in the case of the lady with the cat, they are excellent for actually altering physical conditions and are frequently used to reduce cancer lumps. I always use the technique on myself to speed up the healing process for any knock or blow.

This is one form of what some people call the placebo effect, although the user is aware of the placebo which makes it more useful and usable in many ways; most placebos must be used without the patient's knowledge in order for the technique to work. One of the simplest placebos is to tell someone they are looking better because of something they have done. Their belief in the person who is telling them this can be enough to make them actually become better. Placebos don't have to be sugar pills: whatever form they may take, they are a valuable and important side of healing.

Lifestyle

Sometimes one of the most immediate changes we can make on the 'self-help' front is to change the pattern or form of our day in terms of work, rest and play. Often there is too much work and not enough rest or play. Or sometimes no work, with an excess of leisure time which we cannot enjoy, trained as we are to 'earn our free time'.

Tough as the advice may seem, any bad situation, whatever it is, can always be made better. The first stage is realising that your lifestyle is harmful to you and the second is knowing what to change about it. If you are self-employed with money pressures and a busy work-load, consider your methods and work out basic questions like 'Is the energy output making any money?' or 'Would I be better off packing up and selling bunches of flowers on my doorstep?' If you are unemployed and restless, frustrated and with a large hole in your ego, then go out and give your services free to someone that needs them (social security will do most of the rest). If you are a housewife, perhaps used to having a job and a full social life, and now feeling trapped at home, then start looking at what you have, instead of remembering what 'the old times' were like. Find new interests, push yourself into unlikely pursuits and surprise everyone. Without wanting to write a book on the subject, what I am trying to say is that you can always do something to better your lot. First of all, though, you've got to knock down your own negative thoughts, self-destructive tendencies, excuses, shyness, laziness, stress or whatever is holding you back and keeping you in the well-trodden rut.

STRESS

It is a common myth that only people in high-powered jobs can suffer from stress in its many and varied forms. But from the cradle to the grave we can all be prone to this serious and frequent problem. When we are under pressure, almost anything, be it major or minor, can trigger off a reaction that results in a nervous breakdown or serious illness.

Stress is a chain reaction, where no particular beginning or ending can be determined. Poor nutrition can lead to illness, weakness and stress. A shock can lead to poor nutrition, emotional imbalance, stress and illness. Pregnancy can cause stress, leading to poor nutrition and ill health. And so on. Stress is the body's reaction to a change in lifestyle, and can be either the cause or the result of a long-term deterioration of health.

Whatever the cause of stress, the body's reaction to it is based in the adrenal glands. Healthy adrenal glands produce large amounts of many hormones, such as cortisone, which help to mobilise the nutrients needed to meet the demands of stress. Some hormones cause tissue proteins to be broken down to supply sugar and fat for immediate energy; others pull minerals from the bones; another, known as aldosterone, which controls urine production, holds salt and water in the body, thus increasing the volume of blood and its pressure against the walls of the blood vessels. This increase in blood pressure helps to push into the tissues the nutrients needed to cope with the stress. This is why high blood pressure is so often a symptom of stress. Remember this chain of events can be promoted, initially, by emotional feelings or lack of nutrients, as outlined above.

Another 'by-product' of stress can be the retention of water, which can result in oedema, and the greater the severity of stress, the greater the amount of water held in the tissue. Severe oedema can be a symptom of very long-term and intense stress, indicating that the adrenals are nearing exhaustion: they may well be 'starved' by faulty diet of the nutrients needed to enable them to work properly. And because in the 1980s so many people are subject to such frequent stress, our bodies need more careful nutrition than ever before in history.

16

Other parts of the body affected by stress are the thymus gland (in the neck), the pancreas and the stomach, the latter often giving rise to ulcers. Stress strips the body of Vitamin C and pantothenic acid (part of the Vitamin B complex) in particular; but also calcium, other minerals and vitamins, some proteins, fats and carbohydrates. Very often our nutrition levels are so poor that the needs of the adrenals cannot be met — result, illness.

The Road to Balance

Of all the problems which face us in the modern western world, the effects of stress must rate at the top of the list of ills. It causes both short-term and long-term physical symptoms ranging from headaches to heart troubles, and these debilitate the body, reduce our effectiveness at work and play and can damage or destroy relationships.

As with most problems, it is only when conditions become intolerable that we are forced to make the changes necessary to restore harmony, good health and balance. But with a stress problem, where the causes are not as obvious as they would be with a more tangible illness, the ill health affecting the mind can inhibit self-awareness and the effort to restore balance.

The Family and Friends

The effects of stress are often very clear to those around the person concerned, while the sufferer remains blind, unwilling to admit to a problem 'in the mind', often fighting against all the good advice. He or she often becomes antagonised at attempts to help and can, with a self-destructive attitude (a symptom of depression associated with most forms of stress), actually increase the damage done by food and lifestyle which played a large part in causing the problem in the first place.

Reactions to the effects of stress are as varied as the sum of all the individuals. The warning sign is seeing yourself (or someone you know) behaving in a way that is alien to your (or their) individual and very personal behaviour pattern. This is the time to act. As long as bouts of uncharacteristic behaviour are only occasional, then reason and a positive programme to rebalance the system can be put into action. If stress symptoms are neglected and allowed to become the norm, the sufferer will find it very difficult to face up to the problem and it will be all the harder to restore balance.

Understanding the Problem

Getting to grips with the two critical first steps can be the most difficult action of all: actually saying, 'There is a problem' and developing a true and genuine desire to put things right are crucial to the treatment of any illness.

Stress-related problems exist at the root of most illness, or looking at it in another way, all ill health will produce a stress factor which will help to continue the decline of true health.

Without the full support of our minds we cannot achieve recovery from illness or really good health. This is the nub of the problem: we must all not only understand the external factors of our lifestyle that cause the decline in health, but we must understand ourselves.

All things in the human understanding start and finish in the mind and with the spiritual values of life. This sounds very heavy stuff for simple, everyday people, but don't be frightened or put off by trying to see a little further.

All true understanding is simple

You cannot work with your hands in the soil as I have always done, and not understand the true balance of the forces of nature.

I have often heard the wisest words from those with little formal education who have spent their lives in love with natural forces, learning, as I continue to do every day, that the road out is really very simple. Yet perhaps for those reasons it is difficult to find for many who have allowed their honest values to be replaced by the worship of high technology and 'sophisticated' attitudes.

If we look at our bodies down a microscope we will see only a part of them, that limited view, like the dots that go to make up a photo in a newspaper. With practice we can learn to stand back and view the whole.

It is the view of the whole body in respect of ill health that helps to motivate a complete programme of *rebalancing*.

The common road taken by the conventional approach to diagnosis is to fall into the 'red herring' trap. In an attempt to provide good counselling the most obvious cause is taken as the *root cause*.

Of course the 'obvious' cause of an illness exacerbates the underlying weakness, very often acting as a trigger. A good example would be a particular problem — money worries, job loss, etc — that pushes a person over the edge resulting in a crisis.

A crisis then evokes a crisis reaction: usually the prescribing of powerful drugs to remove the symptoms. This is also often done when there isn't even a crisis. In my experience, powerful doses of valium are often prescribed for minor complaints of worry and tiredness, these doses continuing for ten years or more, as a matter of routine prescription. Today there is more awareness of the

18

problem, and this dangerous situation is resisted by both responsible practitioners and more aware recipients.

However, as conventional medicine has little else to offer but drugs, persistent health problems which bring about repeated visits to the GP usually end in such prescriptions. It is a major problem and my recipes for results, I'm afraid, require an active rather than passive role from the sufferer.

THE BEGINNING OF ACTIVE SELF-HELP

I must assume that by reading, even getting hold of a copy of this book, you feel a degree of positive interest, no matter how unconvinced and sceptical your attitude may be. I ask you to consider, are you experiencing some or all of the following:

a) Shortness of temper
b) Lack of self-confidence
c) Lack of resolve and belief in yourself
d) Depression over little things or nothing at all
e) Lack of patience
f) Frequent headaches
g) Lack of energy, low spots during the day
h) A general feeling of ill health
i) A tendency to look for the high life, to find excitement
j) Outward boldness and confidence, accompanied by inward worries
k) Heavy drinking and smoking
l) Dandruff or skin problems

If you can say honestly yes to any one of the above then it is time you became a living herbalist.

Likewise, if you can detect any of these outward signs in a friend, neighbour, loved one, your awareness can guide them.

If our problems were to vanish with either pill or plant, life would be so easy. Yet the true solution to the removal of damaging illness may not be easy to carry through but it is essentially simple — it just needs a few changes.

I say, and many will endorse this point of view, that *working for the positive balance of the next day is all that matters.* The long-term future is unimportant compared with taking the initial step. If you find after taking the first steps that you experience a feeling of general well-being, you will probably quite naturally want to pursue the matter of healthy living. But it should always be at your own

19

pace, as you slowly and surely become a 'living herbalist'. After that, you can worry about long-term possibilities.

The future is unimportant in terms of both medical treatment and general health. Why? Because in my experience, people live with their bodies on an hour by hour basis, and the further you try to look ahead, the less relevant the action you take becomes, and that all important motivation loses its strength.

So for now forget the fact that you might reap long-term benefits! Any such achievement is a bonus. I want you to feel a little different every day, to be able to measure your progress by an undemanding yardstick. If you aim too high, you will fail and, most importantly, you will fail yourself. And having done so, you will find it much harder to try again.

Living herbalists don't perform some special ritual but live a life as normal to them as any life they had before, but different in that the health of life is valued and respected.

Let me quote here from the experience of a patient of mine, Anne Tayler, whose path to health awareness started with things considered in this chapter:

Our culture has a tendency to consider that 'the ultimate experience' of eating consists of titivating the grossest levels of taste and smell and not worrying what the food is *doing* to you. For me the change from unhealthy eating to a balanced diet has taken about ten years and has been nourished by physical changes that have taken place in me over that time — triggered by my starting to practise Hatha yoga and, more importantly, transcendental meditation.

Just naturally, as fatigue and stress gave way to a wholeness and delicacy of senses, so other aspects of my life had to change, and it happened so gradualy and so 'non-fanatically' that those around me accepted it too. I tell my friends I'm a bit 'picky' and not too keen on meat, but if it's offered to me in good faith I will eat what I'm given. (After all, my liver and kidneys were designed to eradicate toxins: I must give them some exercise!) On the other hand, a little understanding of what some foods *do* to the system is a marvellous stimulant to head towards a balanced diet, and the feeling of getting up from a dinner table feeling better than when you sat down is an enormously satisfying experience. It's also quite amusing when my six-year-old, who can't resist party cakes and chocolates, stuffs himself at parties and then moans because he hasn't enjoyed the food.

With me, good resolutions are useless without the strength of mind to carry them out, and I only started with what felt comfortable or the changes would have caused more stress to the system than benefit. But once I started to grow in awareness and understanding, each new step became easier as the rewards showed themselves in the intense well-being that grows and grows and grows and. . . .

CHAPTER THREE

Nutritional Herbalism

PART I
ENJOYING FOOD THAT IS HEALTH-GIVING

Eating is one of the major pre-occupations of mankind, and early man, like wild creatures now, spent the greater part of his waking hours searching for and eating food. Although in western society this is no longer necessary for our survival, we still spend a lot of time thinking about, buying and preparing food, simply because we enjoy it. Some people enjoy watching advertisements on television for the latest TV dinners and shopping for them the next day. Some like growing their own vegetables, eating, bottling or freezing them. Some love cooking complicated dishes requiring skill and time, or sampling the art of others in their home or in a restaurant; still others enjoy eating fish and chips or a hamburger out of a box on street corners. There are different pleasures associated with all these types of eating, and each brings a different sensation: we eat because we are hungry, because it is a meal-time, to socialise, for something to do, to be comforted, to be rewarded; the list of reasons for eating is endless.

Eating should provide comfort and stimulation and a sense of sharing, but it should also give us all our nutritional and body-building needs. Keeping the body in prime condition helps prevent illness or enables us to deal with disease more rapidly through being equipped to use our natural healing forces. Only in a healthily fed body are these forces potent and readily usable. Vitamins and minerals come from our herbs and food and therefore correct cooking methods are vital to preserve these and the other life forces in food. Many people eat badly, using vitamin pills and other supplements to 'keep fit': this is not the long-term aim of a living herbalist.

The reason eating properly is so vitally important is that it is the easiest way for the average person to control and heal his or her own body, instead of needing to surrender its care to other people's hands. Correct feeding and self-nurturing is our right, thus maintaining emotional and physical well-being. So often we overlook the simplicity of its effectiveness, using the psychoanalyst's couch or powerful drugs instead.

Eating habits: how can we change them, and why should we?

Being told to eat nutritious food because 'it is good for you' is often a hard fact for people to swallow! What proof have we that brown bread is better than white? And if we really dislike brown bread and thoroughly enjoy eating white bread, then what do we do? What value is a healthy diet if the food experience is miserable, the food being prepared with a heavy heart with time-honoured food rituals out of sight?

What we probably need at this stage is a really persuasive 'carrot' to dangle in front of our noses. Maybe I can suggest just that carrot! Sit down and imagine yourself with everything you have ever wanted — a few savings in the bank, a better job, lovely holidays, a beautiful house, a really wonderful relationship with your loved one — or whatever. It may seem bizarre for me to suggest that eating properly can achieve these things, but everything in this world follows a continuous pattern. If because you eat better your headaches disappear, you have more energy, you are a more likeable and sociable person, this could mean you have more to contribute to your job or, if you are unemployed, you may have a better chance of getting a job. You may also find that through balancing your mind and body via eating properly, previous ambitions and goals now seem irrelevant or uninteresting. They are replaced with other, more fundamental and genuinely fulfilling desires, with your own ego and self-interest quite naturally taking a back seat.

You have now read two case histories of patients who discussed the subject of changing their diet. The patient quoted in the introduction did this rapidly and positively due to serious illness; his family followed suit when they found that herbs and healthy food could heal. This man had vital reasons for changing and the family had proof of its importance, but what of other approaches? The second case history (in Chapter 2) showed a slower and more relaxed approach to the question of 'good diet', with the patient experiencing mental changes due to mind and body exercises and finding that her instincts and feelings pointed that way, rather than being forced to change her diet because of ill health. These two examples illustrate the two major reasons for changing to healthy food, but they do have a common factor: the patients somehow managed to enjoy their new-found foods and dietary outlook, which they plan to keep for the rest of their lives.

Everyone has his or her own way of bringing about an education of mind and body, on the food front, but let me give you some simple guidelines, which apply whether you are changing your diet due to illness or for reasons of preventive medicine.

Think what it is like to coax a child or baby to try new foods. You must persuade yourself as you would persuade the baby and wipe your brain clean of preconceptions, mental barriers, apparent dislikes or even strong likes. The word is 'just give it a try', starting very slowly, with a little at a time. If you are switching from white to brown bread then do it one loaf per week, then two loaves per week, and so on until you are only eating wholemeal brown bread. If you are trying to give up tea and coffee then start with the one you like less and cut that down, one cup at a time — but always replace it with something really good. In other words, when ridding yourself of bad habits, don't pick up other ones, go straight to the top, getting your taste buds interested in the very best and healthiest foods. It's often a good idea to psych yourself up for a little while before doing anything. In other words, if it's sugar you are giving up, then say to yourself, 'In three weeks time I'm going to cut sugar out of my diet completely.' During the intervening period think about the project ahead and, if you feel like it, indulge to the hilt while you still have bargaining time!

The withdrawal symptoms from giving up some foods can be quite severe and like any drug addict you are sometimes going to feel a strong urge to return to the drug for a 'lift'. My advice is to give in occasionally, because if you don't, you may give in completely after a while and waste all your efforts. But if you do allow yourself a 'reward', then make sure it doesn't lead to another and another. The bargain with yourself is a reward, occasionally! After some months you will truly find that these pangs disappear and you will probably reach the stage of wondering how on earth you ever consumed those foods in the first place.

After even a few days, and certainly after a few weeks of reforming your diet and taste-buds, you will start noticing why 'brown bread is better than white' or 'coffee is harmful'. Your body will provide answers to your questions, it will start throwing off some toxins and start functioning better, you could experience anything from a lack of constipation or headaches, to just general fitness. However, quite possibly alongside these benefits you might also experience side effects that are not altogether enjoyable. People coming off sugar, coffee or tea suddenly don't have the artificial 'lifts' throughout the day and the body is having to function without these props, drawing on other reserves within the body. Tiredness is hardly surprising, especially if other reserves are low. A 'healing crisis' (see page 67) is even possible. This is often why the 'slowly but surely' method is better than the 'instant and complete' method. However, do not be discouraged. This tiredness or overall low feeling does not last, but it is at this time that you need the greatest amount of mental reserve. Hang on to any periods of tremendous well-being you may experience, and promise yourself that you could very soon feel like that all the time. This is not a hollow promise and there are thousands of people to prove it. Try talking to a few of them.

It is at this point of reforming your diet that herbs are invaluable. Not only do they help flush away toxins from the system, ousting accumulations of mucus in the stomach and bowels, harmful acids and hundreds of other congestions, but they tone, build, feed and strengthen, making the job of the body's 're-conditioning period' far easier and more effective. This is particularly important for old, stubborn and chronic diseases, when the body lacks its own nutritive resources to heal itself entirely. But before we move on to discuss specific herbs and their use, let's look at the harmful effects of some of the foods commonly consumed in this country, alongside some healthy and enjoyable alternatives.

DRINK

The average consumption of tea and coffee in this country is about seven cups of both or either per day. This intake very often reaches fifteen cups per day and fifty cups per day was quoted recently as the intake of a famous politician. Just one cup can cause damage.

Coffee

Due to its irritative qualities coffee can cause anything from cystitis to liver toxicity, and contribute to many hundreds of other, apparently unrelated, conditions. High caffeine consumption also contributes towards the precipitation of acute hyperglycaemia (high blood sugar levels) due to worn out adrenals. This is because coffee strips the adrenal glands (through continually over-activating them) of many things, but in particular two B vitamins, choleine and inositol. This will in turn lower the body's resistance to infection and increase demineralisation of bones. Water retention can occur and the constant robbing of proteins can cause the eating away of our stomach cells, giving us ulcers. Beyond this, caffeine can even produce 'cognitive impairment' (delirium). On top of all this, excessive intake can also contribute to agoraphobia due to continual autonomic activity, giving way to a lower than normal threshold of panic. In all it can induce stress of mind and body. It can also cause insomnia, muscle tremor, restlessness, overworking of the kidneys and bowels (the latter causing constipation) and is often one of the major causes of migraine headaches.

I would not be without coffee in one instance . . . in the First Aid cupboard, as its highly stimulative powers can, in certain situations, be invaluable. Chewed in its raw state or made into a strong, black drink, it can help comatose conditions or reverse other poisons. But it is important to know which poisons it counteracts, because if it were given for poisons which already increase the heart rate dangerously, the result could be catastrophic!

Decaffeinated coffee is not a good substitute as caffeine is only part of coffee's harmful make-up, its acids causing just as much damage.

Tea

One of the most interesting facts about tea and one that surprises most people is that it contains twice as much caffeine as coffee. The misunderstanding of this fact occurred, I think, because coffee was originally made stronger than tea (in the days when tea was expensive) and therefore, one did not consume as much caffeine per cup of tea as of coffee.

The astringent qualities of the tannin content of tea mean it can curb hunger yet stimulate the body due to its caffeine content. Perhaps this is why some people always drink a cup with their meals. However, tannin in even moderate quantities is bad for 'protein digestibility'. (Tannin is also present in coffee, so this fact is relevant to coffee drinkers too.) Both tea and coffee can be labelled anti-nutritional, producing indigestion and low energy levels, 'black tea' being the worst offender. Tannin also inhibits the absorption of iron and the uptake of thiamin (Vitamin B1), a vitally important vitamin for growth, repair and nourishment of the nervous system, among other functions. Not the least of tannin's offensive qualities is that your stomach lining will look just like the inside of your tea-pot!

Green teas from China and Japan have many medicinal qualities in their natural form. However, many deleterious substances such as inorganic salts of copper are added to them for importation. So unless you are in China or Japan, don't drink tea.

Just what do we drink?

Having read about the generally offensive qualities of tea and coffee, I hope that your mind is open to some more beneficial suggestions. Fear not, we can still provide highly stimulating alternatives if that is what you need for the time being, but even the need for constant stimulation should decrease after a short time with some tasty, nutritional herbal teas.

Herbal Teas

Their merits are infinite and they can be enjoyed on every level, because some which are particularly delicious are also beneficial to the body. Those taken for serious medicinal reasons take the place of pills and potions, while still providing an alternative to tea and coffee. There is a herbal tea for every mood, feeling, complaint and illness. They can be used as tea-bags, drunk with ritual in a tea-pot or made up in a flask and taken to work. There is no excuse for not drinking herbal teas on holiday, at work and so on, because they are every bit as convenient as conventional tea and coffee.

Herbal teas are not just a 'drink', they are also a liquid food. A good 'mixed herb tea', made with five or six herbs, can quite safely be drunk instead of a meal occasionally, if time is short. Their strength lies in the fact that they contain so many vitamins and minerals and also aid the assimilation of nutrients in general. A good 'combination' of herbs produces the best herb tea because of the interactions of the various ingredients, where the effect of the whole is greater than the sum of the parts, or where 'more shades of colour' are seen. This is the luxury of having so many thousands of plants to choose from, each with their own numerous uses. With drugs, the active ingredient has been taken away from the rest of the plant and then usually synthesised as well, whereas the active ingredient in a herb is in a living relationship with its other plant substances, all affecting the whole body. This allows for better assimilation with inbuilt safety mechanisms, or, in other words, avoids the side effects that drugs produce. With a 'combination of herbs' the effect of buffering and supporting the action of very dynamic plants becomes all the more possible, safely enabling many systems and organs to be treated all at the same time, producing a better overall result.

Regardless of any outstanding symptoms and damage that the drinking of tea and coffee may have caused, it must always be assumed that there is a general lack of B vitamins, especially B1 and possibly exhausted adrenals, liver and kidneys together with a sluggish digestive and nervous system. (See page 27.) Therefore, a 'general herb tea', designed to rehabilitate the whole body, would be a good choice. I will be giving a great many herbal tea recipes as this book unfolds but here is just one to set your mind working in the right direction. It's very tasty too.

Morning Starter

This tea has invigorating, tonic, feeding and cleansing properties, and is intended to be drunk in the morning to provide a 'lift'. However, many people, including myself, drink it all day long!

This tea can be drunk as a 'beverage' using a tea-bag (one popped into boiling water for 5 minutes) or made in a pot using one ounce of loose herb per pint of boiling water (this is 'medicinal' strength), also allowed to infuse for 15 minutes.

This tea, like others, can be sweetened, not with sugar but rather with honey — preferably on the comb — or, for a change, fructose or real maple syrup. The quantities given show the proportion of each ingredient by weight.

4 parts Dandelion Root　　General nutritive, tonic and very high in easily assimilable minerals, very cleansing and detoxifying to the liver, spleen and kidneys. Stimulates bile and gastric juices and helps to counteract stomach acidity by doing so. It is the safest diuretic in the plant kingdom.

1 part Spearmint　　This adds a lovely flavour to any herbal tea but is generally good for colds, flu, indigestion, cramps and flatulence, affecting the stomach, intestines, muscles and circulation in general.

1 part Yellow Dock　　High in iron and a general nutritive, particularly beneficial in cases of general stomach weakness.

2 parts Sarsaparilla　　An ancient herb, much used by Red Indians and still drunk hot in London streets on cold days. This plant affects the blood, skin, circulation and intestines. It is a powerful tonic and blood purifier, also having anti-putrefaction properties. It contains iron, potassium, chlorides, calcium and magnesium, and aids the kidneys by promoting perspiration and the flow of urine; it contains many hormones which help balance the body and repair the adrenals and therefore the nervous system; and also breaks up and eliminates mucus from the entire system.

3 parts Burdock   A potent, natural antibiotic, this is also a general nutritive and tonic, high in iron. It helps eliminate excess nervous energy brought about by drinking tea and coffee! It also helps decongest the lymphatic system, which is our auto-immune system, aiding our bodies' defence against disease. It is rich in natural hormones which, like sarsparilla, help the adrenals.

2 parts Nettles   High in iron, silicon and potassium and other vitamins and minerals, nettles also help the assimilation of calcium and other important minerals, with a beneficial effect on the lungs, kidneys, bladder and blood in general.

1 part Rosemary   Stimulates the blood stream, dilating blood vessels. It increases the action of the stomach but also acts as a nerve sedative.

1 part Hibiscus   Rich in Vitamin C and malic acid, it is healing to the system in general and lends a very tasty and intriguing flavour to the whole tea.

This tea is further flavoured with Essential Oil of Bergamot Orange, which gives it a very interesting smell. Or just add some lemon juice for taste and blood purification.

Herbal teas and herbal coffees have had a pretty dowdy name in the past and perhaps rightly so. They have generally been given to people because they were 'good' but without proper, up-to-date knowledge of the subject and certainly no idea how to make them tasty and exciting. Things have now changed as a greater variety of herbs is increasingly available. However, if you are buying herbal teas, do choose a good 'combination' which will benefit all parts of the body. It is also more likely to have a pleasant flavour, as many herbs on their own are at best bland and at worst slightly sharp or bitter. Careful blending balances the flavours as well as the many-faceted benefits. Otherwise you can try making your own teas following suggestions in this and many other books.

The Question of Sweetness

I mentioned drinking herbal tea with honey, so let us consider the good and bad points of sugar and other sweeteners.

Sugar

There are many different kinds of sugars available — white, brown, dark brown and so on. The best of the sugars are those still containing molasses which come from countries like Barbados and Guyana, but even these should be eaten with respect. White and brown sugar are generally one and the same thing, the brown merely being the white coloured.

So what is the real hazard of sugar? Firstly, refined sugar contains no food value at all, except calories of course. It goes straight into the bloodstream, raising blood sugar levels very fast. What we get (and we evidently enjoy the experience of sugar, because we always come back for more like a drug addict) is a sugar-rush or hyperactivity. The pancreas strives to rebalance the blood, by removing the sugar into storage. A very 'sugared' body develops, along with a 'trigger happy' pancreas through its constant over-activation, but the result is an almost constantly low blood sugar level or hypoglycaemia. It is a very common problem. Since early childhood we are told that sugar gives us tooth decay but few of us really realise that sugar attacks the calcium in our bones long before it reaches our teeth, the calcium stripped from our bones then deposits itself in muscles, arteries, joints and major organs, which often results in rheumatism and arthritis in later years among other problems. Not only this, but sugar lowers our general resistance to diseases, giving viruses, bacteria and fungi the time of their life! Often problems like thrush and other fungal diseases are a pointer to an over-triggered pancreas.

Honey

Honey off the comb is the best honey one can possibly eat and the darker the colour the better, as it means it is rich in minerals. But beware of honeys that are made with white sugar to keep the bees fed over the winter. Try and find a source where the beekeeper gives the bees back some of their own honey during the winter, or at least feeds them on blackstrap molasses. If possible, buy local, organic, British honey, as imported honey will often have been 'heated' in order to treat bee disease problems and this destroys many of the honey's beneficial properties. Otherwise, honey is a great natural healer, containing antibiotics and a host of nutrients. A sign of excessive honey intake is nausea — unlike sugar, which gives no warning signals. Remember, it is the natural 'whole' sucrose, fructose, vitamins, minerals and enzymes, which are missing from refined sugar, that make honey digestible.

Alternative Sweeteners

A good alternative is fructose, available in healthfood stores — expensive, however, because it is whole natural fruit sugar. For a change, real maple syrup is lovely, but avoid saccharines and cyclamates as they are composed entirely of chemicals. Liquorice is six times as sweet as sugar but has none of the components of any of the other sweeteners. However, it does have a strong flavour which you won't always want. It is an excellent substitute sweetener for diabetics, totally safe. It is lovely added to herb teas and is available in sticks or powdered form. Pure blackstrap molasses has a flavour all its own and is exciting to cook with, especially in cakes and puddings, while malt barley is very rich in B vitamins, nourishing and tasty, and gives yet another sweet flavour.

Chocolate

Giving up chocolate has to follow on from the ban on sugars, but as well as having a harmful sugar content, chocolate itself is a stimulant similar to coffee. Very often what we buy isn't even pure chocolate, but a chemistry set of chocolate-like tastes alongside pernicious additives.

Fruit Juices

As well as herbal teas, drinking natural fruit juices is an important part of one's diet. They make a change from herbal teas and are often most welcome on a hot day. Freshly squeezed grape juice or apple juice is so different from the cartonned, bottled and canned — albeit fresh and natural — version, that there is hardly room for comparison.

Of course, the leap from packaged natural juices to the disgusting, sweet, chemical concoctions called 'squashes' is even more obvious. The latter cause stripping of calcium from the entire body together with hyperactivity and general degeneration of the body. Natural fruit juices are the only juices one should ever consume — and the fresher the better, so if you make your own with a juicer machine, then that is wonderful. As a cheap alternative, wholefood shops do sell 'pure fruit juice concentrates' (which is all that some brands of fruit juices are made from anyway) and these juices have had nothing done to them bar reducing the amount of water to make a concentrate; there is no added sugar or anything else for that matter. To make a drink, simply add water to replace that removed but fruit juice concentrate's usefulness is legion and its price most attractive. The various fruit concentrates are useful for flavouring herbal teas

31

that children find difficult to drink but they are also useful for flavouring food in general. Apple juice is one of the best juices, being highly nutritious and alkaline, also containing potassium.

Water

Tap water is a damaging substance, as it is laced with harmful drugs and chemicals. These include lead, cadmium, pesticides and heavy metals, in fact over 300 harmful organic chemicals in all, not to mention all the drugs that people take which end up unable to be dissolved and are thus recycled into our tap water (that is if water is recycled, as in London and other major towns). Synthetic oestrogen is one example, due to the widespread use of the pill. Ninety per cent of it is dissolved, leaving 10% to build up over a period of time. Even the processes we supposedly use to 'purify' our water of bacterial contaminants are injurious to our health: chlorine, for instance, combines with other chemicals in the water and produces monster chemicals which, among other damaging possibilities, are potentially carcinogenic.

Pure bottled spring waters like Perrier, Vichy and Evian (which have all been 'vetted') are good, if pricy! But they are very useful if you are away from home. At home, water filters are the cheapest and best solution, the safest and cheapest type being the charcoal filters which cost a few pounds to buy and pennies to run. One type, 'Mayrei 2000', just fits over the tap head and can be bought from most wholefood/healthfood stores. I use this make myself — and incidentally it is small enough not to interfere with the washing-up!

Alcohol — its good points

While we're on the subject of drinking, this seems a good time to mention alcohol. Some alcohol in small quantities is actually beneficial and even seems to help against coronary heart diseases by raising the levels of high density lipoproteins in the blood. I am, of course, talking about good quality organic, or better still 'herb based' wines or the odd tipple of good brandy. Or best of all, high proof pure alcohol made from grains, like top quality vodka. It is the cloudy residues in alcohol that are harmful, the worst being Guinness and other stouts. Wine therefore comes somewhere in the middle and spirits at the top of the list. People often assume that it is the high proof that is harmful, but not so. Obviously one's intake must be minimal, although at least two fluid ounces of vodka per day will help to burn up excess hydrochloric acid produced in the stomach. And certainly the relaxing properties of alcohol aid the digestive system and the mind.

32

Alcohol — the bad points

More than three drinks a day of anything is proven to cause liver deterioration, mental problems, birth defects (pregnant women shouldn't consume more than one fluid ounce of vodka per day — or the equivalent — and preferably no alcohol at all), to say nothing of the increased risk of road accidents, social problems and so on. All alcohol may trigger off sexual feelings, but in the long term it impairs potency and lowers testosterone levels in men. As for beer, that supposedly macho drink, it contains a lot of natural oestrogen in the hops and together with its effect on the male hormones, can create female secondary sexual characteristics like breast development in men. Alcohol also vastly increases one's need for many vitamins and minerals, partly because of its diuretic properties which leech the nutrients out.

If over-consumption of alcohol is a serious problem, then you should seek help, possibly from Alcoholics Anonymous. If the problem is not so serious, then a change of diet and some exercises could help to re-balance the mind. Otherwise, a help in weaning even slight alcoholics off drink is the food combination of bananas and a carbohydrate such as wholemeal bread, which bind together to form a chemical called tryptophan in the body. Scientists have discovered that this substance helps to lessen the need and desire for alcohol.

FOODS

White Flours Are Bad

Our next naughty food category are those foods (cakes, biscuits, white bread, etc) based on white flours which have 35% of the original grain removed. The bran and surface endosperm is taken away, leaving creamy white granules (the starchy endosperm of the grain) which are then bleached with chlorine dioxide (the one used to clean toilets, etc). What in fact has happened to this bread is that all the 'best bits' have gone. The natural vitamins, minerals, protein and roughage are removed, leaving behind a sticky, mucus forming, starchy, unstable, 'tasteless', binding mass called white bread, which is still consumed in vast quantities all over the world. Nowadays, the manufacturers do put back certain vitamins and minerals but it still remains vastly inferior to wholemeal bread — especially as the vitamins and minerals are synthetic themselves. White bread became fashionable in the Middle Ages when the rich sought it out for its

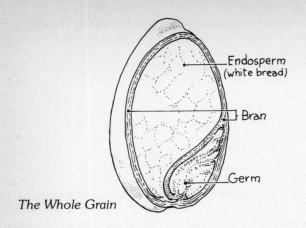

The Whole Grain

apparent purity, thus turning it into a quality product. In fact the story of white bread then was just as horrifying as it is now, as the bakers whitened it with chalk, alum and sometimes arsenic powder or ground up bones from the local graveyard!

White flours are not only used in making bread but in pasta and cakes as well, while white rice falls in the same category as white bread, having had all the goodness removed.

Brown Bread

Synthetic brown bread, cashing in on the uninformed public opinion that brown bread is better for you than white, is perhaps the most dangerous of all. It is made from bleached white flour with brown colouring — usually caramel.

Wheatmeal Bread

This bread has had 19% of the coarsest parts — bran — removed, and, although it is better than ordinary white or brown bread, it should be avoided in favour of wholemeal bread (see below) if possible.

The Alternatives

Organically grown, British grown, stone-ground, wholemeal wheat is the best flour to choose.

To start with, British wheat is much softer than American wheat and therefore contains less gluten, which is the sticky substance in the endosperm of the grain, present in all cereals. Gluten is mucus-forming and can clog and irritate the entire system, especially aggravating the respiratory system and causing asthma, sinusitis and other respiratory diseases. It is also particularly harmful for all nervous illnesses. However, mucus is a substance needed and produced by the body in small quantities to protect its sensitive surfaces, but if our diet is too heavy for our lifestyle and is therefore poorly assimilated or not assimilated at all, as is the case with white bread, then the body throws off the extra in the form of mucus.

Canada and the USA produce high gluten wheat due to their harsher climate, while because of its cheapness most bread in this country — even wholemeal — is made from Canadian wheat. British wheat also contains more protein, and if you can find somewhere where it is grown without the use of sprays, then so much the better. The answer here lies in making your own bread if you have time, or buying from a known and trusted source. Stone-ground flour is better than plain 'wholemeal' flour, because it means that stone has ground the grains instead of steel or roller plate mills, which generate enormous heat due to their speed. This affects the quality of the flour and can cause the wheatgerm to become rancid. Wholegrain flour of the best quality described above contains protein, carbohydrate, calcium, iron, phosphorus, potassium, thiamin, riboflavin, niacin and many vitamins including B and E.

['Hofel' is a trade name of a brand of British grown, organic wheat, among other useful products.]

Wholemeal Flour Alternatives

So often people think in terms of wholemeal flour when considering alternatives to white flour, but there are so many to choose from made from various grains and other parts of plants' seeds. Many of them produce a very much lighter flour, ideal for sauces and cakes, and contain a host of different therapeutic ingredients. Some contain very little gluten or none at all, like soya flour, potato flour, maize flour, mung bean and chickpea flour, rice flour and arrowroot. Rye and buckwheat are lower in gluten than most grains but rye is a very heavy grain and can be constipating in some cases. Millet is the lowest in gluten of all the grains and out of the seven, contains the most vitamins, minerals, nutritives and protein.

Gluten is the binding agent in bread and other foods, but there are many other natural binders. Here are some alternatives all assuring the binding quality necessary for sauces, cakes and bread (but with a very low gluten or no gluten content) producing a very high texture akin to that of white flour.

3 Way Light Flour

For savoury dishes, containing no gluten.
1 oz Maize (Corn) Flour

1 oz Potato Flour
1 oz Rice Flour
2 tsp Arrowroot

Easy Flour
Ground almonds with maize flour — delicious and easy to work with.

Three Way Light Flour
For sweet dishes, has a low gluten level.
1 oz Stone Ground Wholemeal Flour
1 oz Soya Flour (this adds to the natural sweetness)
1 oz Rice Flour
2 tsp Arrowroot

Eating healthily does also mean one can still eat cakes, cookies and so on, but they must be home-made, using these flours, occasionally and for special occasions even using eggs.

Some people, whose bodies are full of toxins, should not eat any glutinous foods at all for a while. This means avoiding all the grains, or, if you must eat them, preparing them in ways which will be less mucus-forming (more about this later in the chapter). However, for most people, grains are a wonderful source of food vitamins, minerals and other nutrients, and anyway they are very enjoyable.

Bran

This is the covering of the grain, consisting mostly of undigestible carbohydrate, cellulose and fibre.

People frequently tell me that they are eating bran for breakfast, happily thinking that they are doing the best for their bodies. It does seem to be the doctor's stock answer to 'roughage'. However, the true story of bran is that it leeches minerals from the body while often causing flatulence. Try the 'Whole Grain Porridge' (see below) or a long pre-soaked muesli as an alternative breakfast. Or if you are eating bran in an attempt to regularise the bowels, then use something like psyllium husks (plantain seed). Taken with water or fruit juice, the husks swell to make a highly absorbent gel which can help carry old or putrefying material out of the colon. This therefore, not only acts as a bowel regulator but also as a colon cleanser. (There is more about care of the bowel in Chapter 5.)

Muesli

Today the fashion for eating cold grain mueslis with fruit and nuts — often with the addition of milk — is quite widespread. These grains are cold and non-alive and need to be woken by a small amount of heat in order to release their valuable elements. For maximum food value, grains should be pre-soaked and/or gently heated. Also the best grains are the whole ones, and in fact the easiest way to cook these is to place your selected grains — whole buckwheat, whole millet, whole barley, whole wheat or whatever — into a large thermos flask, filling it a third full. Top up with boiling water and give it a good shake. Make early evening and leave overnight — in the morning the grains will have opened up and will be soft and tasty. So much nicer and more flavoursome than the dry, slightly tasteless mueslis that we make sometimes. Very often commercial manufacturers resort to the 'very heat-rolled' grains, which are softer and dead, and lots of dried fruits to disguise the dry mouthfuls otherwise experienced! Oats and rye are sometimes difficult to buy 'whole', so use 'stoneground' instead.

This 'Whole Grain Porridge' is so gorgeous and with a little unsalted butter, honey or malted barley it makes a lovely warming breakfast, lunch or tea for at least three-quarters of the year with our climate. You can add dry (pre-soaked) or fresh fruits like banana (always eat when totally ripe and brown, though with the skin unpunctured) or apricot when making it, or even add fruit juice concentrate to the water. For full protein value, sprinkle, with the ground three seed mixture (see page 45). The method for cooking the grains: never let the temperature go above 130°F — this is just enough to allow them to release their goodness (proteins, vitamins and minerals) yet retain them. To prove this point, try sowing some of your porridge in the garden the next day — it will grow! Without heating, the food value will not be unlocked, while overheating destroys it. Anyway, eating *whole* grains unprepared is impossible, as they are hard and indigestible.

Dairy Products

This heading generally causes more concern and apprehension than any other. Surely milk and cheese are among the best foods on this earth? We are told they are often enough on television, by parents and friends, and yet I see more sick people who have over-indulged on dairy products than any other single food grouping. Milk and cheese are particularly damaging to children and they can help cause sinus problems, heart problems, allergies, colds, constipation, chronic fatigue, headaches, obesity and teeth deterioration. One of the points against dairy products is the lactose present in milk, cheese and yoghurt; there is a great deal in milk but a lot becomes pre-digested in cheese and yoghurt-making. Many of us do not have sufficient natural lactose to break the digestible lactose into digestive sugars which are assimilable. Yoghurt, although obviously made from milk and therefore potentially just as harmful as milk, does have the benefit of live yeasts within it. These yeasts are beneficial to the body, but are killed by the addition of fruits (except bananas) or sweeteners (see page 45-6).

Butter, although obviously a dairy product is almost free from mucus-forming substances and can be consumed in small amounts, although it contains roughly 83% fat and 1% protein!

So often cholesterol is the word linked with excesses of dairy foods and heart problems. This may or may not be valid. Cholesterol is in fact made up of fatty crystalline substances and is not easily soluble, although it is necessary at times for the formation of oil in the hair and skin. The problems are caused by over-production of these fatty substances. But most certainly it is xanthine oxidase present in homogenised milk which causes heart problems through hardening of the arteries. Drinking milk in preference to other fluids to quench thirst very often results in obesity and subsequent strain on the heart.

Cheese is even worse, being a concentrated form and very often salted. Migraine headaches are frequently caused by cheese consumption due to the presence of the protein tyramine as well as the generally poor absorption that milk and cheese causes in the body. This is due to many things but one of them is the excessive mucus production (we all need *some* mucus) that is generated by milk and cheese which clogs up the intestines (and other areas). This mucus forms a coating on the inner lining of the stomach and hardens, making an impermeable layer which prevents the absorption of nutrients. This does however vary from person to person depending on their assimilation abilities. It causes similar damage in the bowels, producing chronic constipation. Mucus is such a sticky substance that stools adhere to the colon wall with it and similar problems arise in the respiratory system where chest congestion causes anything from a continually blocked nose to asthma. This excessive mucus production, remember, can also be caused by an imbalanced intake of the many other mucus-forming foods, which really means all foods except raw fruit and vegetables.

Milk and cheese constantly cause allergies like hives and skin rashes because they overstimulate certain stomach cells which produce a hydrochloric acid deficiency resulting in proteins entering the bloodstream. Even if this did not happen, fifty per cent of cows' milk protein is indigestible anyway. These non-fully-digested proteins irritate the tissues and produce a large array of skin irritations and allergies. They also weaken the body generally, making it more prone to hay fever and other allergies — to dust, chocolate, chemical sprays: there are many irritants that can spark off an allergic reaction.

But aren't dairy products rich in calcium, you will be wondering? Indeed they are, but in fact many humans are not able to metabolise that particular form of calcium. Blood tests very often prove this point. Let us look at the proportion of calcium in dairy products as against other foods and we will see that there are many alternative sources, primarily kelp, which is the collective name for seaweeds: made into soups or just taken as tablet supplements, they are a very concentrated form of calcium. Vitamin D must also be present if the body is to absorb calcium properly.

	Calcium (mg)
25 gms (1 oz) hard cheese (also contains Vitamin D)	230
25 gms (1 oz) cottage cheese (also contains Vitamin D)	23
¼ pt Milk (also contains Vitamin D)	170
125 gms (5 oz) Natural Yoghurt (also contains Vitamin D)	250
25 gms (1 oz) Almonds	70
25 gms (1 oz) Watercress	252
25 gms (1 oz) Dried Figs	80
100 gms (4 oz) Sardines canned in oil (also contains Vitamin D)	624
25 gms (1 oz) Kelp (Seaweed)	306

Our daily requirement is about 800 mg per day with sufficient sunshine or other sources of Vitamin D to absorb the calcium. We can get all the calcium we need from kelp tablets and sardines.

Eggs

Very often eggs are thrown in under the heading of dairy products, so it seems wise to discuss them now. Eggs, like milk and cheese, are often the alternative to eating meat for vegetarians. I once made a count of 24 eggs per person per week in a college where a small section of students, including myself, were vegetarians. The cooks had little idea of what to cook and turned to these for a protein substitute! Eggs do contain protein but so do vegetables, grains, beans, nuts and seeds in their correct combinations (in their organic, live state) while the B vitamins often missed in non-meat-eating come from vegetables, herbs and yeasts.

Eggs are a very concentrated form of protein — too much so, in fact. They are also very constipating: don't we use them as binding agents in cooking? Like milk and cheese they are very mucus-forming (gluey and sticky) while cooked eggs deposit inorganic sulphur in the bowel. If you must eat eggs, make it no more than two per week and preferably only the yolks which are the least sticky part. The only eggs worth eating are those coming from chickens running wild and scratching around for worms and minerals with roosters amongst them. Factory chickens and the eggs they produce have little or no food value at all; they are fed on hormones and antibiotics among other things, and cannot digest them — not to mention the pesticides, herbicides and chemical fertilisers they take in with their food. Also the eggs are not fertile as no roosters are present, and this inevitably lowers the nutrient level.

Make a vegetable omelette if you wish, using potato juice (which is high in potassium) to bind it.

Eggs are potential causers of diseases like arthritis, gall stones and kidney stones, and if you suffer from any of these or have a tendency towards them, avoid eggs altogether — they were designed for the baby chick, after all!

There is now available an egg substitute called Bipro which is made from the whey of cheese. It is pure protein and contains no fats, carbohydrates or cholesterol. Worth a try?

Some Dairy Product Alternatives

It is a tremendous misconception that we need lots of animal or animal-related proteins and it seems so hard to change people's minds on this matter. We do need proteins, but few of us realise that the right kinds are found in nuts, roots, seeds and grains. You continually find vegetarians eating vast amounts of dairy foods apparently to sustain their bodies. What we need to know is what kind of protein we need, how much and where to find it. Alternatives to cheese as something to eat for lunch, or make a sandwich with or flavour a sauce with are colossal. Soya and its many food potentials are of major help here — soya milk, soya cheese or tofu, which is a very bland substance easily turned into a cheese dip or salad dressing. If you do eat cheese, at least make sure it is natural, fresh cheese, not processed in any way.

Soya milk itself is a very concentrated form of protein and should therefore be used fairly sparingly — and certainly it should never be drunk as one might drink milk. It can cause allergies of its own! I use it occasionally and usually water it down. Once the container is opened it lasts for three days in the fridge and makes a marvellous alternative to milk in sauces and puddings. Always buy the unsugared brands.

There is now a very tasty dried form of soya milk available. It is called 'Soyviter' and is produced by 'Healthiers' — useful if you only use it occasionally and in small quantities.

Instead of cheese with bread at lunchtime, think about peanut butter — in the sort you buy in healthfood shops the peanuts have merely been ground down and contain no sugar or preservatives. Coming from the whole peanut it is high in protein, as are hazelnut and other nut spreads, sesame seed spread and so on — the latter is also rich in iron. Of course it may not be protein as such that you are after, if you consume enough of it at other times of the day. Sprouted beans and seeds are nutritional powerhouses (see pages 45-47), or try tomatoes or beetroot for an array of vitamins and minerals; sardines in oil, very high in calcium as shown on the chart earlier. Or what could be better than a cucumber sandwich?

I am often asked if goats' milk is a good substitute for cows' milk. Although similar in many ways, goats' milk is unpasteurised and immediately scores over cows' milk as far as harmful mucus-forming is concerned. It is a nutritious source of raw protein and is much finer and more digestible than cows' milk, with smaller fat globules. It is also richer in simple fatty acids, is naturally homogenised and has a higher phosphate level — useful to vegetarian diets. Also useful to vegetarians, it has a higher Vitamin B1 content than cows' milk — above all, it does make a very tasty cheese and yoghurt which can be eaten occasionally. As far as the milk is concerned, if a little is just about okay, then more is *not* good. There is now dried goats' milk available, useful for the odd occasion, or in small quantities.

How do I bind if not with eggs?

The traditional binding elements in food are eggs and flour. Other excellent binders are things that may surprise you, all of which contain little or no gluten. The potato has one of the strongest binding properties and one can use the water from boiled potatoes (with their skin on) or use the whole potato mashed and sieved (having been steam cooked). This is the traditional base for a lot of European sauces and soups and in fact in Belgium only vegetable sauces are made, using potatoes, tomatoes, herbs etc., which are then liquidised or sieved. They make much more interesting, tasty and healthy alternatives to fish or cauliflower cheese sauces! If you do have difficulty getting something to bind or firm up then there is no better herb to use than arrowroot. A healing plant in its own right (and excellent for convalescents), its mucilaginous and softening qualities are soothing and digestive, and of course it contains little or no gluten. If a slightly spicy thickener is required then try ground coriander, but it is not nearly as thickening as arrowroot.

Meat — The Big Con

The theory that meat ensures a healthy diet with plenty of protein is just as false as the myth that dairy products are vital to our well-being. But it is important to understand what the alternatives are, as a little knowledge can be very dangerous in this context. If you know your commitment to getting alternative sources of protein will be half-hearted, then wean yourself off meat, fish and dairy products slowly, or just partially, cutting out the most harmful elements first. This will lead you on to a more and more healthy diet, as your body and mind come to feel better and more lively. But do not force yourself into extreme measures so that you become depressed and therefore ill in the process.

Protein

We've been talking about proteins a lot, so let's consider them in more detail. Too much protein is in fact harmful, yet we do need amino acids for our metabolic processes — growth, repair and the production of hormones and enzymes. Yet an excess of amino acids — which are the basic component of all proteins — forces an elimination or 'shedding' of very important trace elements like zinc, calcium, magnesium, iron and chromium, all vital for emotional and physical well-being top to toe. The shedding of calcium, among other harms, seems to point to the fragile bones of the elderly.

If you are going to eat meat and fish then you should only consume a maximum of one and a half pounds of flesh foods per week (3½ oz/100 gms per day). For less active or non-growing bodies this could be reduced by about half. All meat dishes, particularly red meats, increase the likelihood of uric acid forming in our bodies and causing the evils of arthritis and rheumatism. However, having said this, a 'balanced' intake of protein in some form is essential, as a totally non-meat diet without due care and attention to alternative protein intake, with the careful combining of essential amino acids, is just as dangerous as an excess of protein. Too low a consumption of protein will produce very visible symptoms like allergic sensitivity, bronchial and nasal congestion (lots of clear mucus), tiredness, cold extremities etc, etc; these symptoms could continue for as long as one to two years after you change to a better diet. Having been an 'uninformed vegetarian' myself for many years I know this to be absolutely true.

42

Half to two-thirds of daily protein intake should be consumed at breakfast time, to give us energy by raising the blood sugar levels. This is easy and enjoyable when you know how, but you'll have to forget the old idea of toast and marmalade for breakfast, with steak and two vegetables in the evening.

The worst meats are the very red ones such as beef, which are not only full of steroids, formaldehyde and other anti-spoilage serums, antibiotics and hormones (as most farmed meats are) but they also contain high quantities of creatine, a member of the caffeine and theine family (the two stimulative and toxic elements of coffee and tea) all of which are heart and kidney stimulants. Pork is very high in fat (67.4% on average) and very low in protein (only about 9.4%), so in fact one is consuming almost all fat. All meat putrefies in the intestine and generally strips calcium from the body.

The *fatness* of meat is an important factor in its digestibility and a certain amount is important for essential fatty acids, to prevent dry skin etc., but olive oil and other vegetable fats are preferable. Excessive fats raise cholesterol and uric acid levels in the tissues and they also interfere with the proper metabolism of carbohydrates and encourage diabetes. Too much also dulls the brain by causing clogging of capillaries, reducing the amount of available oxygen. The list is endless.

Offal

Kidneys, liver and heart, all being dense structures, are very hard to digest, while liver and kidney contain nuclein (a substance closely allied to uric acid). All the toxins that have not been excreted by the animals on killing are also stored in these organs, so we are taking in the toxins with the meat.

White Flesh

If you are going to consume flesh then the white meats are better, especially if they are fed on natural grains and greens (not steroid feeds) and have had plenty of grazing room. Chicken and turkey come into this category, having far less stimulative properties, while a little lamb occasionally could also be put into this bracket as it has only 28% fat, 17.6% protein on average. Most lambs roam free over untamed countryside like the Welsh hillsides and Australian outback.

Fish

This is also one of the better flesh foods, although the poisoning of our oceans with radiation and heavy metal accumulations now also puts its consumption into the 'risk' bracket. Avoid shellfish as they are 'bottom of the sea feeders', generally the most toxic as they consume the rubbish of the sea. Fish which are not bottom feeders are the best, as they avoid the pollutants which tend to drop to the bottom of the ocean. Cod is a good choice as it is high in protein and low in fat. Strangely enough, fish like farmed trout are probably the most free from chemical waste and toxins, but again find out what they have been fed on and what kind of waters they swim in. The other good point about fish is its Vitamin D content, the vital vitamin for calcium and sugar metabolism.

Just remember one thing about meat, and that is that most animals live on the bounties of nature to produce their own fine health and muscles; we are quite capable of doing the same. Think also about the way the animal has been killed, with all the fear and adrenalin pumping around the body at the kill. We are absorbing those fear vibrations — no small matter.

Disguising the Facts

Always try to buy meat in an unprocessed state i.e. avoiding sausages, minces etc. Apart from having a lot of fat content they are often made from the older, poorer and normally more toxic parts of meat, while the mind is also diverted from the fact that you are eating flesh as it is chopped or shaped beyond recognition. So often I see people who are squeamish about looking at a dead chicken, insides 'n' all, but who quite happily tuck into hamburgers and sausages; this has to be wrong.

Protein Alternatives

One of the major alternative sources of protein is avocado (which also contains Vitamin B12). When I suggest this, people always wince and say how much they cost. But if you use them as a main meal protein substitute for meat, shilling for shilling you are undoubtedly spending far less and that is if you eat the whole avocado — they are very filling!

Spirulina protein should not be taken by those with high blood pressure and should only be used occasionally as a supplement, never instead of a meal. It is a blue/green algae and is higher in protein than almost any other food. It also contains high quantities of Vitamin B12 — much more so than liver — as well as Vitamin A, iron and more. Being low in bulking qualities, it is a wonderful source of protein for slimmers, mostly due to an amino acid present in it that acts on the brain to suppress appetite. Spirulina is best taken in tablet form — three before each meal — while vegetables, seeds and roots should be consumed at the meal as a substitute for other high protein foods like nuts. Spirulina makes an excellent recuperative supplement for those who are suffering from protein deficiency, especially vegetarians and vegans who have failed to balance their diet properly.

Broad Beans and Whole Rice

This combination deserves a heading all of its own due to the fact that combined, they provide the full range of the amino acids — all 22 of them — needed to form a whole protein. Amino acids are organic acids which are the building blocks of protein. These proteins are then converted into hair, skin, enzymes, hormones or whatever in the body, as I mentioned before.

It is a very useful combination to know and even if some of the vitamins and minerals are killed off by freezing these foods, the amino acids are not and they make, therefore, a tasty, all-year-round meal. Any combination of grain and legume is highly beneficial, in fact.

Seeds for Protein, Vitamins, Minerals and Nutrients

Sunflower, pumpkin and sesame seeds mixed together produce a complete protein (i.e. they contain the eight out of the known 22 amino acids that cannot be made by the body); they are also rich in essential fatty acids, encourage the production of certain enzymes, and contain many of the B vitamins. Compared with steak they have three and a half times as much iron, twice as much protein and 25 times as much thiamine, with lots of Vitamin E. Always store them in the refrigerator. Use them as a salad base, or liquidise them and use to sprinkle on food, or as a sauce ingredient over cauliflower or stir-fry vegetables. As these are rich in protein and some fats they should however be eaten in moderation.

Drumsticks or Urd Bean

Difficult to obtain except in Indian populated areas, this long 'vanilla-pod'-like bean has more protein than any other vegetable. It does, however, need a lot of gentle cooking. When eating, the soft, slimy contents should be sucked out like marrow from a bone, discarding the hard, indigestible outer skin.

Yoghurt

This is the most easily digested protein of all and the only alkaline animal food; it also encourages bacterial flora essential for digestion. An overly acidic diet destroys all this flora, as antibiotics and other drugs do.

Technically, you should eat twelve to fourteen ounces of yoghurt at a time! This is an awful lot, but some will be killed by stomach acids, leaving much less than that to do the job of establishing good digestive flora. Also remember, however, not to combine it with anything except banana, the three seed mix or wheatgerm, so as not to kill the culture. You can also add torula yeast or lecithin granules. Be sure to buy only 'live' yoghurt, as much 'natural' yoghurt has had its acidopholous (yeast) killed off in order to give it shelf life. (A diet high in sprouted seeds and grains can replace the need for bacterial flora and Vitamin B supplements.)

Cottage cheese

This is one of the lightest cheeses and it does contain protein. Although this is an acid protein and not ideal, it does provide some relief for cheese addicts!

Nuts, Grains, Seeds and Legumes

These also contain large quantities of protein, fats and nutrients — this applies particularly to all nuts to many of the grains, especially millet. However these should all be combined together, or at least some together, in order to make a complete protein. Remember also that they make a complete protein when slightly cooked (as in the flask method, p. 37). These are all concentrated foods and should be eaten frequently but in small quantities (say two or three nuts at a time). Nuts do deteriorate very quickly once out of their shells, and should be eaten soon after shelling. They certainly should not be eaten if at all rancid.

The B12 Factor

Many people believe that if you don't eat meat you will be low on Vitamin B12, but I have listed many protein sources which also contain B12. Another source which also contains many other vitamins, minerals and nutritives is sprouted seeds and beans.

Sprouting Seeds and Beans

This is a very cheap and easy way of gaining all your necessary vitamins and minerals, which in turn increase the assimilation of other nutrients. It supplies us with alive food all year round and squashes any excuse that salads are expensive out of season. It also opens up people's horizons, showing that a salad can be more than two pieces of lettuce, tomato, cucumber and lots of mayonnaise. Soaking seeds, like flask cooking the whole grains, is a way of making them release their goodness. Seeds, grains and pulses can be treated in this way and if it is done properly it can increase their vitamin content some 700%. This includes Vitamins A, B complex, B12, C, E and many more. No need for the vitamin pills!

How to Sprout
You can either buy a sprouter from a wholefood or healthfood store, which gives excellent instructions on the container, or you can use old glass sweet jars or jam jars. Put a handful of seeds, grains or pulses (seeds are quickest) in the jar, fill it with cold water, cover with cheesecloth and leave overnight. In the morning pour off the water through the cheesecloth and then turn the jar upside down to drain off any excess water. Do this twice a day. In three to five days you will have sprouted seeds, roughly the length of a small fingernail. Once sprouted, rinse three or four times and then add lemon juice to stop oxidation and loss of Vitamin E and to take away pungency. Always keep a regular supply going and refrigerate any not in use. Stir-fry into other vegetables, use in salads, mix with baked beans for children or just liquidise with soya milk and water and use as a convalescent or pick-me-up drink.

One tablespoon of sprouted grain is equal to three pounds of steak in enzyme value.

RAW FOODS (AND DRINKS)

A diet consisting of about 75% raw food has excellent rejuvenative qualities and helps to reinstate what should be our natural balance of 80% alkaline to 20% acidic — most people are almost all acid! This sort of diet throws off toxins, removes mucus build-ups by increasing oxygenation and elimination of stored toxins, as well as increasing the metabolic rate generally, which is very helpful to weight loss. Used when dealing with the early stages of a healing programme this ratio should be altered later. (See page 51 for suggested percentage intake.)

Raw Fresh Vegetables and Fruit Juices

The greatest authority on this subject is N. W. Walker, D.Sc. and his book *Fresh Vegetable and Fruit Juices* is well worth buying and reading.

Just like bean, seed and grain sprouting, these juices can provide all our missing and vital organic minerals and salts and consequently our vitamins. By 'juicing' the vegetables and fruits one is keeping the vitamin, mineral and fluid content while discarding the fibre. This means that the goodness of the alkaline vegetables or fruit can be assimilated in the body in about 15 minutes instead of hours. Who would chomp through ten raw carrots, five sticks of raw celery and two raw beetroots at one sitting anyway? You couldn't; your digestive juices wouldn't be up to it. The juicing process also unlocks a lot of the food value which can remain permanently locked up in the 'whole' raw vegetables, whose molecular structure is just too binding. For instance, the Vitamin A in carrots is not surrendered except in light steaming or juicing of the vegetable. But any cooking kills many enzymes and nutritional food values, also changing the food from alkaline to acid. However, fibre, as everyone knows, is vitally important to one's diet for peristaltic movement and cleaning the intestines, so sufficient 'whole' raw food must be eaten as well. Many people assume that because the juice is removed from its fibre it is concentrated and therefore possibly harmful; not so. A concentrate is something that has had its water content removed, which is not the case here. These juices are some of the least concentrated foods yet the most nourishing, and their health-giving results are very rapid. As a matter of fact, white sugar is 4200% more concentrated than carrot juice! Carrot and beetroot are respectively high in Vitamins A and E whose combination will heal almost any wound — a useful twosome to know.

The Living Elements

Live, vital, organic elements are essential for repair and proper functioning of the body, and this is why vegetables and fruit juices are an infinitely preferable form of mineral and vitamin sufficiency to the synthetic pill version, which is often overloaded with buffers, colourants, preservatives, mordants and other horrors. A good gardener will know that vegetable and fruits are only worthy of the soil they are grown in. So selective and careful buying or growing of them is important, as only a soil rich in nutrients itself will produce nutrient-rich food. Of course, as a living herbalist you should ideally grow these foods yourself; this in turn provides another essential factor — that vegetables and fruit in season are better for one's system and 'balance'.

When and How to Use the Juices

You can use these juices in very small quantities as a daily maintenance programme or in higher quantities in times of stress, when you are undertaking a healing programme. I tell all my patients to buy a juicer machine as a vital companion to eating raw foods in

48

general. They are useful if a patient starts to lose too much weight after giving up sugar, white flour, chocolate, etc. The juices will stabilise the patient's weight in a matter of days while allowing maximum elimination of toxins. They are also useful in the case of what I call 'Western Malnutrition', a common complaint in this country, when a person is chronically anaemic, tired and ill, due to a diet with no real food value. Juices provide speedy and foolproof rehabilitation. My own juicer is a fairly mediocre affair but good enough: the really good ones cost a lot of money and are mostly sold in America. Please do not mix juicers up with liquidisers — they are quite different pieces of machinery. (See pages 65-6.)

It is best to consult N. W. Walker's book for many hundreds of vegetable and fruit juice combinations to sort out a range of problems including arthritis, obesity, high and low blood pressure, boils, lack of sleep and many more.

I am going to deal with the subject of fasting in more detail below, but let me say here that after a fast, fruit and vegetable juices (freshly drunk at the time of juicing, which is always the golden rule) are a good way of re-introducing the body to eating again. It is a gentle re-introduction, quickly providing easily assimilable nutrients and giving instant energy. The television tells us that Mars bars give us instant energy, well I'm telling you that vegetable juices do!

THE USES OF FASTING

Removing excess mucus from the body is important. What is mucus? It is a normal secretion of the body's mucus membranes to keep the lining of the throat, nose and alimentary canal and other sensitive surfaces lubricated. Excessive production caused by foods is different from 'normal' mucus which should be transparent and slippery. It is thick, sticky and cloudy and contains many gel-like substances to which dirt and toxins are attracted. This kind of mucus is produced all over the body — in the digestive system, lymphatic system, lungs, bowel, reproductive system and connective tissues. I have mentioned the harms of mucus before, in connection with high mucus-forming foods like dairy products, high protein flesh foods, eggs and white flour. One way of ridding ourselves of mucus build-ups and other toxins is sensible fasting. It also removes the 'food' of infection.

A one day fast on grapefruit or oranges is excellent for removing mucus and other toxins from the system, grilled oranges being particularly anti-viral. This is a vital process as all the good food and herbs in the world may never be absorbed if the hard, old, encrusted layers of impermeable mucus and other resistant toxins are left to encase the stomach lining. This process is quite dramatic and may not suit some people, especially as an enema may be necessary to relieve the body of toxins further by their speedy release. But there are slower and more gentle methods.

A one day grapefruit fast is the equivalent of a twelve day total fast. Eat one medium-sized grapefruit with its pith, gently grilled, at 8 a.m., noon, 4 p.m. and 8 p.m. Acupuncture or acupressure will further stimulate the production of hydrochloric acid, which will have been suppressed if excess dairy products have been eaten, but the fast on its own will accomplish much. Consult your natural practitioner before doing this.

Dr Christopher's 'three day cleanse' is a fasting programme based on drinking fruit juices for three days. It is worked out as part of an overall eight-week plan and is a wonderful way of detoxifying the body ready for healing and regeneration. Over the three days, three gallons of toxic lymph are eliminated and replaced by three gallons of alkaline juices! The process is quite tough and sometimes very painful — but well worth it. (For more information and for other food and recipe guidelines, see Dr Christopher's book *Regenerative Diet.*)

A seven-day grape fast followed by raw foods is of proven benefit: grapes are high in Vitamin A, the healing vitamin. They are also almost pure fructose and need very little digesting.

Fasting Once a Week

This gives the body time to rest, shut down and do some repair work. Choose a day when you have to do little or no work — the same day each week. The mind has a chance to rest and relax, as well as the body, and the fast makes eating afterwards all the more pleasurable! Drink firstly a glass of prune juice and then only purified water with a little cayenne or apple cider vinegar or lemon juice in it and a teaspoon or more of olive oil to cleanse the toxins from the liver. This can be a little hard on an empty stomach. You can also drink blood cleansing teas (see page 117).

The next day, make your first foods fruit, your next vegetables, building up to grains and the heavier proteins towards the end of the day. (Normally the reverse is suggested as a daily pattern.)

There is a ten day fast which will cure almost anything and is useful to know if no outside help is available. Dr Singha, a teacher of mine, has used it often. Drink hot water with honey and as much paprika as you can cope with, as often as possible all day for ten days.

Intuitive Fasting

This kind follows no rules, you just follow your mind when it says I'm not hungry, I don't want to eat, even though it's a meal time. This can be for a meal or for a day, provided no-one is offended or put out by it. As meals are important social occasions too, only you can decide when this is convenient. This kind of fasting is part of the lives of children and animals, the former losing the ability through being forced to eat in order to conform or please. Never eat when you are excessively tired or angry or upset or when you are feeling overworked, depressed or whatever. Always eat when you are feeling relaxed and balanced.

FOOD BALANCE

Understanding the philosphy of food balance is vitally important and until this has been fully grasped it is almost pointless giving out recipes, diet sheets or regimes.

The foods that are essential for healthy living can be split into three main categories.

The Primary Category: Whole Grains

Remember to combine these with beans or legumes to balance the protein (amino acid) content. These should make up 40-60% of your diet.

You'll remember that I discussed the combination of rice and broad beans as being the only one that contains all 22 amino acids (page 45). There are many other grain and bean combinations: whole rice, whole wheat, whole oats, whole millet, whole barley, whole rye, whole corn, whole buckwheat can all be cooked by my flask method (see page 37), either with the addition of aduki, soya or other beans, or with pre-soaked fruits as a sweet alternative.

These primary combinations are extremely balanced between Yin and Yang, with a combination of about 60% brown rice and 40% broad beans being the most balanced of all. This food combination is healing, comforting and very sustaining.

The Secondary Category: Fresh, Organic Vegetables

Preferably home-grown or local and in season, these should make up 30-40% of your diet.

This secondary grouping provides our vitamin, mineral and general nutritive needs, but they are less balanced than the grains, being

51

more Yin than Yang, especially if eaten raw. For this reason, and because of their eliminative qualities, they should only make up this smaller percentage of the diet. They should generally be slightly cooked (under 130°F) to unlock many nutrients. It is the eliminative qualities that make vegetables and fruit so important in a healing programme, often making up 75% of the diet. However, no patient should ever be left on this diet for long, as excessive elimination will leave the body weak and cold, resulting eventually in an excess of water.

Seaweed, high in vitamins, minerals and other nutrients, belongs in this category, as do many herbs which I will deal with at length later on.

The Tertiary Category: Meat, Eggs, Dairy Products and Fruit

This should only make up 10-20% of your diet.

Fruit is a very Yin food while all the others in this category are Yang, and because of this imbalance they should be taken at most in very small quantities, especially dairy products. Meat, eggs and dairy products are high in protein and low in fibre, heating to the body and very stressful to the major organs because of the detoxifying work they cause. Always combine them, therefore, with vegetables and grains.

Fruit is very cooling, detoxifying and strongly eliminative. When the body's temperature is at its highest (usually in the middle of the day), it is a good time to eat raw or slightly cooked fruits. Excessive fruit-eating, especially in the early morning and late evening can overcool the body and imbalance the organs.

A Balance within a Balance: the Three Way Salad

A balanced salad is not always possible, especially if one is sticking to locally grown, in season vegetables, leaves and herbs. But if the ingredients are available, then this three way salad is best.

Take one root vegetable (grated horseradish — Yang);

One fruit or vegetable bulb or stem (chopped green peppers, celery, avocado — also for protein — combining Yin and Yang);

One leafy vegetable (lettuce, watercress, chives, dandelion leaves or parsley — Yin).

Add two tablespoons of sprouted seeds, which contain a balance of Yin and Yang. A perfectly balanced salad.

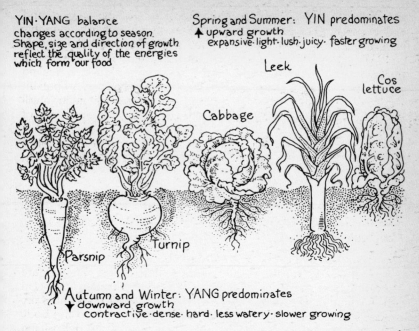

YIN·YANG balance changes according to season. Shape, size and direction of growth reflect the quality of the energies which form our food

Spring and Summer: YIN predominates
↑ upward growth
expansive· light· lush· juicy· faster growing

Leek

Cos lettuce

Cabbage

Parsnip

Turnip

Autumn and Winter: YANG predominates
↓ downward growth
contractive· dense· hard· less watery· slower growing

All vegetables are more Yin than Yang, yet within all Yin there is Yang, and vice versa. Tomato is very Yin, being watery and cooling; horseradish would be very Yang, as it is a root and hot.

The Importance of the Time of Day

At breakfast, the body needs to 'fuel' itself for the rest of the day and breakfast should contain substantial amounts of protein, carbohydrate and other essential nutrients, as whole grain porridges and mueslis do. They are warming and comforting to a body that is not yet fully functioning.

By lunch time the body should be fully stimulated and warmed up and at its most active. Therefore a cooling meal of raw foods like salad is a good idea; add a hot vegetable soup in winter. Sufficient protein, carbohydrates, vitamins and minerals to carry on the afternoon's work should be present. Excessive eating in the middle of the day makes digestion hard and work even harder!

In the evening the body and air temperature are cooling down, so a cooked, warming meal is necessary. It should not, however, be eaten later than eight o'clock. It *should* be relatively light, although social habits tend to make it heavier than necessary! However, remember that the digestive organs are now ready to rest, like the rest of the body, so eat nearer to six o'clock if the meal is a heavy one.

Supplements to the Diet

Additions to this very basic diet outline include kelp tablets (available from Gerard House) for calcium, iodine and natural vitamins; brewers' yeast tablets for many of the B vitamins. Morning or evening take a teaspoon of apple cider vinegar in water with a pinch of cayenne pepper if possible. Fresh apples, nibbles of mixed nuts or fruits are good, but eat them at set times to give your digestive juices time to rest and work to their best abilities when needed.

Other requirements are *specific to each individual, and personal advice should be sought.* For some people this sort of diet would not be correct because of their particular illness, but generally indigestion and flatulence are a sign that one's diet or methods of cooking are at fault.

PART II

GENERAL FOOD AND HERB COMBINATION TIPS

The Salt Question

Common table and sea salts are Yang foods and should be avoided; as they create adrenal exhaustion or 'nerves'. As an alternative, try bio-salt (organic salt) — which is very strong and should be used sparingly; kelp (powdered seaweed); or vecon, a Marmite-like spread made from vegetable salts.

Most of our bodies' salt requirement occurs naturally in raw vegetables, along with potassium and magnesium, but add a little natural salt towards the end of cooking, as salt is lost in cooking and this helps maintain the sodium/magnesium/potassium balance. It also stops food burning. Adding salt too early slows the cooking process.

Rice and meat, however, contain very little salt, so it is important to add it to maintain the magnesium/sodium balance in the body. An imbalance can lead to congestion, kidney disfunction, wind fermentation and loss of magnesium, zinc and copper.

Salt helps to balance the pH (acid/alkaline) value in the body, but always add a little of something sweet, too. Asfetida and salt eaten with legumes help prevent indigestion and wind.

A possible reason why salt has become such a general 'taboo' is that, if mixed with commonly taken drugs like antibiotics and sleeping pills, it increases their harmful side effects. Beyond this, our generally stressed lives do create more stress-related illnesses like high blood pressure, which salt exacerbates.

Cooking Beans

All beans and other legumes should have come out of their glutinous substances and should be slimy in order to be fully cooked. It is important that they be well cooked to avoid flatulence. Add a little ginger and garlic when cooking lentils to help avoid 'wind' problems.

Cutting Your Food for Flavour

Chopping food into rounds produces the mildest flavour, with lengthways chopping giving a slightly stronger taste. Chopping very finely in all directions produces the strongest flavour. Varying the way you chop will not only produce different flavours but, of course, will also create different shapes for visual interest.

The Effects of Cooking Food

Correct cooking of food does not kill it; rather, it makes it more digestible and assimilable. Using heat, pressure, time and salt (all aids to cooking) does make food more Yang and can drastically alter its Yin/Yang character. For example, steaming is much less Yang than baking, though both do make food more Yang.

Oils

Cook with refined oils such as refined olive oil.

For salads, use first and second pressings which are the best quality ones, being the least refined and therefore tastiest and highest in nutritional value.

Remember that there are many oils to choose from: refined oils include maize and vegetable oil and corn oil; cottonseed oil, hazelnut oil and walnut oil are good alternatives — there are twelve in all.

Lemon Juice

This is alkaline in its reaction to the body and therefore good for bodies which are generally too acidic. Added to potatoes, mushrooms or other food likely to turn brown, it halts the oxidation process which destroys Vitamin E. It is one of the best blood purifiers in the kitchen — lemon tea will help any condition.

Pepper

White pepper produces acids; use it only as a seed to flavour, but do not eat.

Black pepper should always be freshly ground and added after the food has been cooked; cooking changes its chemistry so that it becomes more aggressive to the stomach. Black pepper is a natural preservative, anti-catarrhal, anti-mucus, anti-fungal, anti-bacterial. It is a Yang food.

Good Combinations

Good combinations are important as they mean that food will be digested properly and indigestion will not occur. 'Stagger' your meal if necessary. Proteins and starches should be eaten with minerals — ideally vegetables.

Beware of these combinations, which will not help digestion, however good the food is:

a) Protein and starches — eat protein at the beginning of the meal and starches at the end;
b) Fats and starches — e.g. fried bread;
c) Fats and proteins — e.g. steak and baked potato;
d) Fruit and proteins — fruit becomes trapped and ferments in the stomach;
e) Raw fruit and vegetables — raw fruit is very eliminative and can be digested quickly; while raw vegetables are tougher, more earthy and need more digesting. If you eat them together the digestive juices will not get around to the vegetables. It is better to eat them separately, finishing with the sweet, easy-to-digest fruit — this will even enhance the digestion of the raw vegetables.

Indigestion

This is caused by the digestive juices having to go in too many directions in order to digest all the different combinations, resulting in some foods being left undigested, causing pain and wind. Proteins need three hours in the stomach, while fruits go through almost directly. Dill and peppermint tea can soothe a great deal. This is why you must be kind to your stomach and 'stagger' your intake.

56

Puddings

A little sweet pudding is always a good idea at the end of a meal, even if your are feeling full, because the stimulus of the new flavour — sweet as opposed to savoury — will produce more saliva. Fresh pineapple or pawpaw if available is the best at doing this job because of its strongly digestive enzyme.

Re-Heating Food

Always transfer food to another pan to avoid burning of the food due to sediment on the bottom. But always be sure to remove all the food as the best bits are at the bottom! It is never advisable to reheat fish.

KITCHEN HERBS, SPICES AND CURRIES — SUPERMARKET HERBALISM

The Taste of Herbs

Something too *pungent* and therefore unbalanced will produce toxins, discomfort and indigestion, although pungency in moderation will be 'dispersing' to the body. A *sweet* taste is nutritive and feeding, while a *sour* taste is digestive and cooling. *Bitter* herbs are cooling and detoxifying and therefore have a strong influence on the liver. *Salty* tastes affect water balance and digestion, often preventing wind.

Curries

These are very good for you, cleansing the system, forcing out toxins by increasing perspiration, yet curing things like night sweats i.e. balancing the body's sweating process. Uncooked spices are better than cooked but not nearly so enjoyable — and do remember anyway that the rules for medicine are slightly different from those for cooking.

Most spices are good for preventing and relieving gas, also aiding digestion through stimulation. They also help to relieve nervousness, spasms and cold. They are the first line of defence for acute ailments in the first stages and can treat a wide range of problems, which is another reason why the average layman can become a living herbalist.

The common culinary herbs not only add flavour but provide

natural antibiotics, digestive stimulants and just like the spices should always be growing in the garden or sitting dried on the kitchen shelf.

Turmeric is the basis of a curry, giving it its golden colour. It is a Yin spice and an excellent cleanser to the liver, due to its bitter taste. It is also highly antiseptic and as a blood purifier is good for eczema, pimples etc. It is helpful for all circulatory problems and menstruation regularity.

Coriander — Queen of Spices: as a seed, this is a cooling spice, ideal for balance in a hot curry, and a good thickener. It is stimulative, digestive and anti-aphrodisiac! Whole it is sour, while its fresh leaves enhance and bring out flavours.

Fenugreek: one of the most versatile of seed spices, this is tonic, astringent, yet soothing (ideal for ulcers). It contains natural hormones, is anti-diabetic and again is a very useful thickener in foods. Use the fresh leaves chopped on to potato with a little butter.

Aniseed is a sweet spice and useful for a sweet/sour combination. It is excellent for breaking up mucus in the body, and relieves griping in the bowels, also colic and flatulence. Lovely in a curry or just added to a sauce.

Cinnamon is available as bark, shoots and sticks. The bark is sweet, slightly hot and bitter; the shoot tastes very different, not so hot and bitter. It is a Yin herb.

Cinnamon and whole barley grain soup is a diuretic combination and good for all kidney problems, while cinnamon and cloves go very well together in all cooking. Cinnamon is not only lovely in cooking sweet and savoury dishes, but also delicious added to herbal teas.

Nutmeg and Mace: mace is the outer covering of the nutmeg and the two should be cooked together if possible. As a team they are a good aphrodisiac, though in large quantities they can be hallucinatory. Nutmeg is also abortive in large quantities. Nutmeg and lettuce soup is very good for depression and nervous disorders, while mace is an antiseptic and is lovely in sweet dishes. Sprinkle nutmeg or mace on cooked fruit, or use with cinnamon in cakes.

Garlic: this is alterative, stimulant, antibiotic, nervine, carminative and much more. The fresh juice is very effective for cramps, spasms and seizures. Combine it with ginger, French tarragon or marjoram to prevent wind. Combined with onions in soups it is very beneficial for colds and flu, but should not be boiled or it will lose much of its goodness. Chop garlic and marjoram together, sprinkle on toast and lightly grill — lovely!

Caraway: an excellent aid to digestion and for relief of indigestion. Lovely sprinkled on bread or cakes.

Cardamon: the king of spices. Warms the body and is again useful for indigestion and gas. The seeds are aphrodisiac for both male and female, black for women and white for men. Add to dandelion coffee with fennel for a really lovely flavour.

Cumin: another essential ingredient in curry making and one of the best spices for the relief of flatulence, although an excess will filter through the body and make one smell! However, it is particularly useful with cooked beans and fried foods. It is also a stimulant and antispasmodic, of use to the heart and uterus.

Cloves are stimulative and effective in warming the body, increasing circulation, improving digestion, helping nausea and vomiting. Allspice is very similar. Use sparingly as the flavour is strong. They are lovely combined with cinnamon. Combine with cinnamon and turmeric when cooking rice.

Ginger is one of the most versatile herbal stimulants (Yang) and of great benefit to the intestines, circulation and stomach. It enhances the effect of all other herbs and spices. Use a lot of it in soups, stews, curries, breads, cakes and teas. Make your own ginger honey (or buy it from Epicure) and eat instead of marmalade.

Marjoram: stimulant, antispasmodic, antiseptic and carminative, it can be used for cramps, nausea and sickness and adds a lovely lemony flavour to all dishes.

Sage: antispasmodic, antiseptic, astringent and helpful for slowing fluid secretions, it is thus helpful in excessive perspiration, night sweats, milk flow and vaginal discharge. It has a slightly bitter taste, so use sparingly, ideally with slightly fatty foods or when roasting meat.

Thyme is useful in cases of lack of appetite, chronic gastritis and diarrhoea; it is also highly antiseptic and lovely combined in almost any foods, salads, stews, soups etc. Excessive amounts can cause depression but I use it in small amounts at almost every meal.

Rosemary is astringent, highly stimulant, antiseptic, useful in indigestion, colic, nausea, gas, nervousness and fever. It is also high in assimilable calcium. Bitter in taste, it should be used sparingly; it's lovely on potatoes, but avoid it in salads.

Mustard and Mustard Seed: the seed is stimulant, alterative and rubeficient, in all being excellent for the digestive system, aiding the digestion of any food it is combined with.

The best mustards are those which are still whole grain and made with apple cider vinegar rather than white wine or malt vinegar. Use mustard as you would butter, e.g. a knob on baked potatoes, also frequently combine in salad dressings.

Note: As you have probably realised, foods and spices in their different states — fresh, whole, powdered, etc — all have different flavours. Whole, unprocessed spices last the longest, so if you are buying powdered ones, buy small quantities at a time.

FOOD LORE

Many people claim to have a good healthy diet because they eat natural foods. But not all foods sold as 'natural' are as healthy as you might at first think; they may also not be eaten in the right combinations, or may contain too much or too little protein, all because of insufficient knowledge of nutrition. This can result in a number of ailments or diseases and generally totally surprises the patient.

Weight Control

This is a subject rarely mentioned when dealing with eating wholefoods in a balanced way, as a balanced diet will always bring about a balanced weight. With the right herbs to help the situation, this can be done safely and reasonably quickly. (See Chapter 4.)

Nutritional Supplements, Bottled Vitamins and Minerals

These are concentrated forms of food and should never replace primary foods. They can make the mind lazy, foster a lack of interest in 'real, growing food' and take away the important social aspect of eating. A survey has been carried out noting that women in the higher income and 'class' bracket, with more access to money and education, actually come off worse due to their continual use of vitamins, self-prescribed. Firstly their own defence mechanisms are made less potent, but secondly and more importantly in some ways, the effect of the vitamins makes the body feel superficially healthy, so it is unable or less able to give warning signals about chronic or deep-seated illness. In other words, the normal 'feeling poorly' which tells you that something is wrong is disguised.

Excessive taking of vitamins and minerals can in some cases show up as constipation, especially excessive iron intake. Children react very quickly, producing hard, dark-coloured stools.

However, vitamins are often vital in a healing recuperation period and occasionally necessary on a life-long basis, but only if used 'as well as' and not 'instead of', and prescribed by a practitioner. For instance, excessive quantities of Vitamin C can eventually produce a deficiency of Vitamins A and E.

Nowadays we do tend to need more supplements than we used to, with our 'high stress' lives burning up our vitamins and minerals at a much faster rate. However, with our factory farming methods producing a generally lower food value due to soil exhaustion, we cannot always count on the soil producing our needs. After all, all the plants' mineral and vitamin contents depend on the soil they are grown in. With purely organically grown vegetables and herbs we will, of course, have sufficient food value. Having said this, though, many non-organic farmers spend a lot of money each year on feeding the soil with non-organic minerals and nutrients in order to produce 'good' saleable healthy crops. It is, after all, in their interests. Even though I'm against eating foods produced in this way, at least the plant has partially turned some of these nutrients into an assimilable form — more assimilable, I often feel, than inorganic (not changed by the plants at all) synthetic vitamins and minerals, especially the cheaper ones, which can damage major organs by producing toxic build-ups, hindering instead of helping the body. If you do want to use vitamins and minerals or have been advised to, then buy expensive ones made from natural ingredients and natural buffers, mordants, colouring, sweeteners, etc. Choose those minerals that have been chelated (combined with protein to aid assimilation, as happens in nature) in order to make absorption much easier. Good makes are Nature's Flow, Gerard House and the Cantassium Company.

Stress does mean you need extra vitamin and mineral help, especially calcium and magnesium — but also Vitamins C, A, D and E. So take extra kelp tablets for calcium, plus lots of rosehip tea and watercress for Vitamin C, lots of carrot juice for A, oily fish for calcium, magnesium and Vitamin D and wheatgerm oil and beetroot juice for Vitamin E. The whole grain porridge will provide many vitamins, minerals and trace elements, including magnesium and B vitamins. This is a fine alternative to the vitamin and mineral jar! Beyond the extra requirements of stress, the normal daily intake of sprouted seeds and beans (especially alfalfa), good balanced eating and the drinking of herbal teas will all provide high volume vitamin and mineral needs.

Grow Your Own

Wherever and whenever possible it is a living herbalist's obligation to grow his or her own food; obviously the more, the better, but even some parsley and thyme growing in a window box is at least an attempt 'to feel the soil'.

Cooking Boredom

This is a problem shared by more people than one might at first suspect.

Try always to surprise yourself and others while appreciating even very slight flavour changes — no two meals can ever be the same, after all!

Rules

The fact is there are really none. Recipe book rules are there to be broken, if this will encourage imaginative cooking or spur enthusiasm, which otherwise might produce constraint and repression.

The other fact to be remembered is that food which suits one person very likely won't suit the next. The man eating bad food yet releasing toxins quickly through a physical outdoor job will be in far better health than the man eating the same food and sitting in the office all day — he is likely to succumb to an array of illnesses, major and minor. This can be observed in other cultures and countries where almost 'mono-diets' of bad things exist, things which would be highly harmful to most western bodies, like dairy products. These have little effect on their strong healthy bodies used to hard physical work and a segregated environment. The Maasai in Africa are a good example. Likewise some Chinese have a generally very unhealthy diet with lots of white rice, white bread and Coca Cola! Yet their psyche and mental balance, their strong bodies and their use of herbs give them something which western bodies just don't have.

There is one rule, however, that should be observed, and that is: 'If a little is good, then more is not necessarily better.' As always, understanding food values and balance is the vital thing.

Eating Out

Going to friends, being taken to a restaurant, one way or another we're all involved in eating experiences that may be far from the dietary road that we would choose to travel. However, most of the time I can happily pick my way round the majority of restaurant menus and find quite a bit to eat that won't conflict vastly with my

62

desires and ideas on food, yet which on the face of it doesn't look as if I'm doing anything different from everybody else — which is making a choice. The important thing is to make the decision about eating out before you accept the invitation, not once you are at the table. With friends things are usually made a little easier for you — but if they aren't completely like-minded always put them at their ease otherwise the evening will be strained and unrelaxed as they try to produce 'healthy food'. Much better to tell them to cook their normal fare and enjoy the love they have put into it, the value of which never can be counted.

If you feel you really are going to be unwell over something you have foolishly eaten, then 'fast' the next day, eating lots of fresh parsley and drinking apple juice. Also take lots of exercise, in order to release the toxins more rapidly.

SHOPPING

In the course of this chapter you may well have been introduced to unfamiliar foods, so here are some of the places you can obtain the ingredients for healthy eating.

Wholefood Shops

These will probably be the shops you use most often, as generally their range of foods is the most extensive, basic, wholesome and cheap. Also on the whole there are generally very helpful people serving in them. (In the USA they are not only helpful but knowledgeable and highly trained, and can help and advise about purchases, extending your education on the subject.) Very often they sell books on wholefoods and these can be bought alongside the foods.

Healthfood Shops

Very useful occasionally as they often stock things that wholefood shops don't — including a very large range of useful books, as well as things like herbal teas and supplements. But their prices on everyday foods do tend to be higher and the foods not so 'basic', while advice behind the counter fluctuates wildly between complete ignorance and unhelpfulness and tremendous helpfulness and care.

Nationality Shops

These generally reflect the local food requirements and specialised needs of different races and groups. They offer an exciting and wide range of foods, Indian, Chinese, etc. but tend to be scattered and then concentrated! So some areas will not be lucky enough to have these.

Local Stalls

If you don't grow your own food, these are often the next best thing, as the vegetables are at least from soil of your own locality. As I have said before, cheap, local, in season foods are always preferable to exotic, expensive, foreign ones!

Supermarkets

Many people assume these are black-listed, but this is not always so, as the few tins of food and other standard items allowed can be bought cheaply from these places; good quality sardines in oil, baked beans, tomato concentrate, unsalted butter to name but some, so don't turn your back on them but, like everywhere else, read labels! Increasingly major supermarkets such as Waitrose, Marks & Spencer and Sainsbury's are beginning to stock whole grains, live yoghurts, soya milk and so on.

KITCHEN EQUIPMENT

Nowadays there is much more technology concerned with kitchen equipment than ever before, with electric egg-boilers, electric chip-makers, microwave ovens becoming commonplace. It's often difficult to know what's necessary and how to spend your money. Always avoid aluminium equipment, though, as aluminium imparts its particles and a decidedly metallic flavour to food being cooked in it.

Beyond normal requirements, specialised items I find useful include:

A *Wok* for stir-frying vegetables which are later mixed with rice and therefore require a large open pan with a lid.

A *Water Purifier* which is not really cooking equipment as such, but certainly something you should have in the kitchen. The cheapest is the charcoal filter type which fits over the tap — Mayrei 2000 is one suitable make. There are also 'jug' type ones which are useful for offices and other places where you do not have access to a tap.

A *Liquidiser* for pureeing vegetables to make vegetable sauces or easy-to-digest soups. Also for fruit sauces and puddings.

A bamboo steamer

Charcoal water purifier (fitting over the tap)

Vegetable and fruit juicer

The 'plug-in' slow cooker

A liquidiser

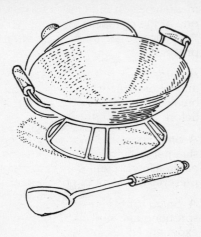

A wok (there are also less traditional, 'non-stick' ones)

top up with boiling water

⅓ full of grain

A food flask

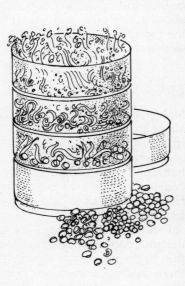

A salad sprouter

A *Juicer* for juicing vegetables and fruit. Unlike a liquidiser this machine separates the fibre from the rest of the fruit or vegetable. It can be bought from an electrical shop or large store and there are many types on offer. My own is a Moulinex 140 Liquidora No. 2 — one of the cheaper kinds!

A juicer attachment can often be bought if you have a food processor.

A *Large Flask* is useful for the 'flask method' of cooking rice, beans and whole grains. The 'food flask' is wider necked and less likely to break but doesn't 'cook' so well; so give it more time and pre-heat before use.

A *Steamer:* there are many types and I have an oriental bamboo steamer costing only a few pounds which has several stacking layers, easily allowing me to cook enough vegetables for the family. They preserve all vitamins and minerals.

A *Salad Sprouter:* this has a three-decked layer allowing easy sprouting and preventing problems of rotting which are sometimes experienced using the jam-jar and muslin cloth method. Cheap to buy and easy to use.

A *Slow Cooker:* These 'plug in' casserole cookers are incredibly economical to use and those fitted with a switch to prevent heating above 130°F will ensure wholesome food. You can prepare food in the morning and it will be ready to eat when you come home from work in the evening.

Other Kitchen Equipment

Many people have pressure cookers; I advise against these as although they do cook quickly they harm the food by altering its structure and over-cooking, destroying most nutrients.

Another novelty today is the microwave oven. This is no more harmful than an ordinary oven, merely speeding the process up by cooking from the inside to the out instead of the outside to in. However, its intense heat (like a hot oven) does indeed spoil much food value.

Freezers are useful on occasions but their very low temperatures destroy much food value, killing their vital, alive qualities. Not only this, but many vegetables need to be blanched in order to freeze them, and this immediately destroys all their goodness. However, they are useful for leftover food should there be any!

FOOD AND 'THE LAW OF CURE' OR 'HEALING CRISIS'

Getting worse before one gets better is perhaps a little Victorian in sentiment but, properly understood, makes sense in natural healing. Changing one's diet, fasting and the taking of herbs, together with experiencing other forms of natural therapies all do one good — they stimulate the body to shed toxins (just a change of diet can do this), winkling out old and lingering rubbish, liberating the body for cleaner living! This elimination process can be quite forceful and of course care must be taken with those who have chronic diseases (they must reach an acute stage to be rid of all toxins), as a body which is already rather weak and degenerated cannot withstand as much positive force as a body fundamentally healthy with an acute illness.

So, therefore, a healing crisis must be monitored and special care taken. Generally the healing crisis takes the form of aches and pains relevant to the disease or diseases the patient is suffering from but occasionally it also reflects patterns of illness right back to childhood. Illness comes from the outside and must be returned there! However, the subject of a 'healing crisis' is quite a complicated one, so it is always best to relate to a practitioner over this. Steps may sometimes need to be taken to slow down or speed up the process, even occasionally delaying it for a while. However, if you do experience it, it does mean that good and positive steps are being made towards good health, although many patients find it hard to grasp that blotchier skin and increased spots or whatever are actually making them better, conditioned as we are to suppressing illness.

I'm closing this chapter with a story from another patient of mine; it tells its own tale. I frequently hear doctors of conventional medicine refusing to believe that good diet is in anyway fundamental to preventing illness. Only recently on television (during a programme on healthy living) did a doctor, a so-called 'nutritional expert', categorically disagree that careful food combinations were an important part of avoiding indigestion, fermentation, wind and general eating discomfort. And on the radio recently, I heard a doctor say of the diet question, 'My job is to heal the sick, not discuss nutrition'. So don't take my word for the importance of diet; here is the story of my patient, Mr Graham Eldridge of Ipswich, written in April 1984.

I first came into contact with Jill Davies when attending a training

68

course for teachers in connection with a twelfth century history project. Ms Davies was invited to give a lecture on herbal remedies of the times, as part of the project. I was greatly impressed by the way in which the relevance of herbs as effective healing remedies for the present age as well as for those far off days was so clearly and cogently presented.

I am at present head of a small primary school in rural Suffolk and of all the teaching posts I have held during eighteen years of teaching, including teaching in social priority areas in Inner London, I would consider that the present post has caused me the least amount of mental strain! However, during 1982, increasingly over a period of months, I began to have more and more quite severe dizzy spells followed by a feeling of nausea, which lasted more or less the rest of the day. You can imagine the difficulties of being a class teacher in this situation — having to 'pitch and sway' to the staffroom and try and get a message to another teacher to ask if they would watch the class while I recovered — which at times could take fifteen to twenty minutes!

I went to see my GP who explained to me that the dizziness was caused by the fluid in the canals of the inner ears being out of balance. He prescribed tablets to try and correct this malfunction. However, despite the dosage being stepped up to the maximum the dizzy spells continued, making teaching more and more difficult and often impossible. It was at this point that I remembered Jill Davies and her herbs — so I made an appointment to see her.

Having examined my ears and discussed my dizziness problems with me Ms Davies together with another professional colleague asked me about my diet, which was mainly white bread, cakes, school dinners etc, and they explained the steps I had to take in order to get better; which included massaging ear drops into the ear for a few months among other things. Before I could get better, I would have to stop eating some glutinous foods and change my diet in general. I had to cut out milk, cheese and eggs completely and replace drinks such as tea and coffee with herb tea. To be told this was no great horror — the dizzy spells had made me feel so wretched that I was prepared to do almost anything for the prospect of getting better and avoiding the confirmation of Meniers disease.

I have kept to my diet fairly well — cutting out butter (eating soya margarine), milk (using soya milk instead) and eggs, and it has honestly not been too difficult. I have also stopped drinking tea, and coffee in particular. Occasionally I have lapses and eat something which I know is really unsuitable, such as salted peanuts — but I'm quickly reprimanded by the younger members of my family!

The change to my health has been enormous — I hardly ever have a dizzy spell and if I do it is only momentary, and I can put the reasons for this down to a moment of dietary weakness like drinking a cup of coffee or eating something which is on the restricted list. I haven't had a single dizzy spell while at school since consulting Jill Davies, for which my colleagues and I are profoundly grateful! Not only that, but I can also dig and tend my own garden, which had become impossible. I have also learned the importance of 'breathing' in yoga and am exploring self-realisation through it.

Realising that the dietary restrictions might be considered by some as being a bit of a sacrifice (although in my view profoundly worthwhile in the long-term) I haven't overtly sought to evangelise others with regard to natural healing methods. However, friends, colleagues and relatives have seen the difference natural healing methods have made to me; the quantity of coffee drunk at playtimes has noticeably diminished, more and more herbal tea is turning up in the staffroom cupboard and the popularity of sticky puddings has in fact declined over the past twelve months!

I can only agree with Mr Eldridge's last comment — seek not to change others; just concentrate on improving yourself and you'll be surprised how even the toughest of systems change around you!

CHAPTER FOUR

Getting Help with your Healing

THE FIRST AND MOST DIFFICULT STEPS TOWARDS HEALTH

As a living herbalist's main aim is to be healthy, it might now be wise to describe 'good health'. It is a common theory — and one that modern medicine tends to foster — that good health is simply the absence of disease. What *I* mean by good health occurs when the body is in a balanced state, totally harmonised and in tune with itself and all that surrounds it. To be in perfect health we would probably have to have had a spiritual experience or be the Dalai Lama, but we can all experience that all round 'lift' occasionally — look at the glow which radiates from some pregnant women caring for the unborn child. To make it more possible for more of us to experience this for more of the time, means following natural healing methods. We must always be aware of the potential of disease, but also of the potential for total health which disease brings. In other words, it isn't a matter of the body attaining 'apparent' health in the fastest possible time, which is the aim of powerful drugs and antibiotics. It is more

71

important to grow slowly, teaching one's body on a minute by minute basis, with the daily growing mentally and physically towards better health making all disease less likely.

The Normal Road

The normal road to take when one becomes ill is either to muddle through on one's own or, if the illness is a little more severe, to go to the doctor and surrender one's body to the prescribed treatment. Both courses of action may or may not succeed in making the illness disappear; but the patient is still left in a state of ignorance about what caused it and how to go about preventing a repeat performance! Let me illustrate this by taking some very common complaints and going through allopathic or conventional medicine's viewpoint, as against natural healing methods. Let us start with the most common disease of mankind:

The Cold

Symptoms: Usually a slight rise in bodily temperature, chilly sensations and an overall feeling of ill health. Generally there is a marked increase in mucus production resulting in sneezing and the necessity to blow one's nose very often.

Some Standard Treatments: A slug of whisky. Lemon squeezed into water with an aspirin. Aspirin, a hot bath and bed to sweat it out.

All these approaches may, each in their own way, eventually ease the uncomfortable symptoms of a cold, yet none either minimises the length of the cold, nor prevents a future possibility of one, by doing something about the cause of it. Most people accept the face value and inevitability of a cold, without thinking any more about it.

The Causes of a Cold: Most people talk about 'catching a cold' and it *is* an infectious disease. Cold germs will go to those bodies which provide the surroundings they enjoy, bodies which are full of toxins and rubbish. The cold ('viral' or 'bacterial' infection) feeds on excessive secretions of mucus which are the waste materials of the body. I described in Chapter 3 the foods (cheese, milk, starches, etc) that produce excessive mucus in bodies unable to assimilate them. Therefore to prevent a likelihood of future colds one needs to follow a much less 'mucusful diet' — as well as ridding oneself of old mucus build-ups. A clean bowel and clean skin are also fundamental factors. A cold can, of course, be due to outside factors — getting wet; improper clothing producing a chill; wearing synthetic fibres which do not allow the body to breathe, especially important if it is sweating. But even with these external causes one can make the outcome less severe. The important thing is to minimise the length of the cold, yet let it take its natural course by clearing out toxins. What most conventional drugs do for a cold is suppress the elimination of toxins, locking in the harmful condition and making sure it will cause more illness later on!

The Natural Way

The most important point about natural treatment is to catch the cold early, at the first sign of chilliness, fever or even the warning signal of inflamed glands. A very famous anti-cold procedure (including the treatment of flu or general fever) is to combine elderflower, peppermint and parsley into a tea, or to use red raspberry leaves or boneset herb as single herb teas. All these teas will produce copious perspiration as well as necessary nutrients like Vitamin C, calcium, Vitamin A and other minerals, vitamins and trace elements which are essential in combatting this condition. Of course, the patient should go to bed. A little time in bed at the beginning will prevent days of later illness and totally destroy the argument of, 'Oh, I haven't got time to go to bed.' I do sympathise with this attitude, though, as family or job commitments are high on most people's list of priorities. So what I suggest is that you go to bed as soon as possible — immediately after work, or as soon as the children are in bed — by six o'clock if possible. Use the evening and night for your herb taking and recuperative period in a positive way.

Another golden rule is not to eat, as eating will only produce more germs for the cold to feed on and take energy away from the healing efforts as it tries to digest the food. Most importantly, make sure that the bowels and other elimination channels are working properly as any constipation will obviously slow down the removal of germs and toxins.

The patient may feel better within a day, or even hours, but it is important to continue treatment after the symptoms have gone, to help prevent a recurrence of the disease.

The Cough

Symptoms: A sudden expulsion of air from the lungs which can produce a single cough or small coughing attack. This is sometimes combined with a sore throat, and can be the result of a neglected cold.

Some Standard Treatments: Most coughs are ignored, especially if they are not too serious. However, if they interfere with sleeping, most people take decongestants or expectorants or throat lubricants, all of which go under the heading of cough mixtures. If you have a sore throat as well, then mild antibiotics may even be prescribed. Although they ease the symptoms for a while, none of these treatments actually changes the real condition or approaches the cause. Normal and perhaps very harmful eating patterns generally continue, likewise constipation or any other degenerative signals are generally ignored, as they have little apparent connection with a cough.

The Causes of a Cough: A cough as described above is the body's attempt to dislodge mucus from the breathing passages, often including the bronchial tubes. A sore throat accompanied by a cough is usually caused by the sinuses draining down the eustachian tubes, which is like pouring acid down the throat. Mucus, as we discussed with the cold, is the major culprit, so the spotlight should be on diet with great attention to the stomach. You should also consider the possibility of general body weakness, lack of sleep, lack of exercise and fresh air, and general insufficient 'all-round elimination', as any poisons and waste matter stored in the body increase the likelihood of a cough. Coughs and colds are rare if the whole system is in good condition.

The Natural Way

Try a cough syrup of honey and onions, using herbs like wild cherry bark, aniseed, sage, liquorice, lobelia and red raspberry, which all provide natural expectorants, demulcents and lubricants. The aim is to break up mucus and phlegm in order to discharge it throughout the whole system. If you develop a sore throat, then the sinuses need to be cleaned out and here, grated horseradish steeped in apple cider vinegar is an excellent remedy. If seizures are experienced then sedative herbs (in tincture form) are best massaged into the chest and lung area, and, as with the cold, the treatment should last well into the period of renewed health. All exercise of the lungs through deep breathing and exercise will open up the bronchial air passages, making the cleaning process of the lungs and the clearing of the cough far more easy.

I mentioned the removal of tonsils in Chapter 1 and perhaps therefore, I should explain exactly why I said that removing tonsils to cure tonsillitis was about as sensible as cutting off one's head because of a headache. It will serve as a final illustration of the differing approaches to the treatment of common illness.

Tonsillitis

Symptoms: A very uncomfortable lumpy swollen feeling in the throat due to the inflammation of the tonsils. There is acute catarrhal infection shown by the redness and swelling of the tonsils which can be seen when the mouth is open. Occasionally there will be ulcers on the tonsils. There is often a chilly feeling and fever, accompanied by a dry throat and mouth and swollen glands.

Some Standard Treatments: The situation, unless it becomes frequent and severe, is usually ignored because most people, including doctors, do not understand the causes of tonsillitis or how to deal with it. If the bouts of inflammation become too frequent and the patient appears to be very ill, then very often the tonsils are surgically removed. Prior to this, large doses of antibiotics are given, often to no avail, generally further lowering the body's defence mechanisms. The real problem is that doctors attach the label 'tonsillitis' to a person, which means the patient must have a standard treatment, rather than looking at the patient as an individual and wondering why *he* has this disease and how it was caused. Without this individual treatment, the patient will never learn how to prevent making the same mistake again in connection with another part of the body.

The Causes of Tonsillitis: Tonsils are one of the first lines of defence in the body and their job is to defend the body against germs. If toxins and wastes accumulate to such a level that germs are frequent, then they can easily become overworked. We are back to good diet, adequate rest and exercise immediately! Tonsils are the filtering system for the whole body and are in fact very important to the body, although we are frequently told by conventional medicine that like the appendix they are useless. Cutting out the tonsils merely lessens the body's ability to defend itself against germ attack; it also destroys a very vital 'warning signal' for us. Not only this, but if the tonsils are removed in childhood it can make puberty far more difficult for both sexes. Their 'filtering' is particularly important for the reproductive organs. Menstruation in girls will be harder and for boys prostate malfunction is far more likely. Not to mention other possible problems in later life connected with the reproductive systems: even childbirth can be made easier because of less toxic waste in the body if the tonsils remain.

The Natural Way

As usual the spotlight falls first on diet. A three day fast on either unsweetened fruit juices or a mono-diet of a fruit, with lots of rest and plenty of fresh air, is the best way to tackle tonsillitis. Together with this, elimination channels must be kept open (if even one elimination channel is blocked more problems will occur and the present problem is compounded); if necessary use herbs to do this. Suitable herbs such as mullein, lobelia and red raspberry can be drunk as tea or made up as a fomentation and placed on the neck. Lymph drainage, massage and reflexology and the taking of tissue salts are some of the many directions one can go to aid recovery.

Having now established the different road that natural healing takes, you will have begun to realise that natural healing methods take much more time and effort than going to the doctor; although generally the illness is less protracted, yet treatment should be continued even after the disease has abated. The recurrence of similar or more severe ill health is also far less likely. After all, as I have said before, it is badly treated acute illnesses that produce all our chronic illnesses. Apart from passing on genetic weaknesses, we really have to blame the present conventional medical system and the ignorance of most laymen for the abundance of chronic diseases of twenty to thirty years' standing. So how do we go about getting help to guide us through our health problems?

Seeking a Practitioner

Finding a good practitioner is becoming increasingly easy as the movement towards natural healing grows stronger. Yet there is no central licensing or registration body for alternative medicine practitioners (except in one district in London . . . so far), nor are they controlled by the state. This I feel is a good thing, as many brilliant practitioners have been trained abroad and might not conform to state qualifications in this country. However, this has the drawback that it does not entirely protect the patient — but in my experience any 'quack' or incompetent practitioner just doesn't survive long. After all, if someone is parting with money and the service is bad, the practice will die a quick death. So in fact the word 'registered' or 'consultant' applied to a natural practitioner only means that he/she is registered with a professional association.

My first suggestion is to seek out and listen to local opinion or ask friends about a good practitioner in your area: a good reputation is sure to reach your ears sooner or later. This is the most satisfactory way to find a practitioner — I run my own practice like this and have never advertised. Very often your local healthfood or wholefood store will be able to put you in touch with somebody.

If word of mouth does not succeed, then try the Yellow Pages — most practitioners list themselves, but of course a string of letters after a name may mean little or nothing to you. If you do not have a personal recommendation, check whether or not the practitioner belongs to a professional association. These bind their members (who are accepted for membership on the strength of their qualifications and abilities) by strict codes of ethics and practice as well as uniting the profession in general.

Or read some health magazines which have advertisements in the back, although practitioners are limited to 'business card' style listings and are not allowed to give full details of the therapies they can offer, or the conditions they are particularly able to treat. This is due to British advertisement regulations and is mainly enforced to stop people making unjustified claims — which I personally feel is a good thing. If a practitioner is worth making claims for, this is best left to satisfied patients. However, this does have the disadvantage that the potential new patient does not glean as much information as might be useful.

Both these approaches are like a 'blind date', which can be a bad experience for both practitioner and patient. Unless you are prepared to take this risk I suggest you go along to an alternative medicine exhibition where it is possible actually to talk to practitioners informally. You can then choose the one you found it easiest to relate to. Otherwise, most clinics or natural healing set-ups are only too happy to talk to you prior to treatment, giving you the option of backing out or 'coming back another day' if you feel the time, or the practitioner, is not quite right. Certainly it is important both that the healer/teacher is happy about the patient/pupil and vice versa, as otherwise time and money will be wasted on both sides.

A practitioner will make a careful diagnosis, which will most likely be slightly different from your own and encompass the whole body instead of a section of it. This will then ensure that you receive exactly the right treatment. When you are ill, your levels of confidence and resolution are often greatly lowered and therefore to have someone helping you through it all is vital for most people. One of the basic ingredients in the practice of healing is listening — so often people literally have no one who will listen to them. When a patient talks about illness, he or she is beginning to release tensions and the negative record in the mind is slowly unwinding. Fears and doubts can begin to change to hope and creativity just through talking about them — and as all this is going on, the chemistry of the body is changing, every cell of the physical body is beginning to function better: some healing has already taken place!

Cost

This is sometimes a thorny question, although I find more and more that people are happy to pay a small amount now rather than pay in terms of a removed bowel section or whatever later on. An average payment for a one-hour consultation is between £10 and £20 plus VAT (which natural medicine, unlike conventional medicine, is subject to). Some practitioners obviously have more overheads, treatments, equipment and staff to pay for, and this will be reflected in the fee. You will have the cost of herbs and herbal preparations on top of the consultation fee, but this can be pretty minimal if you grow them yourself.

The Case History: Looking and Touching

On your first visit to your chosen practitioner, you will probably be asked first of all to summarise your life since babyhood; talk about health, ill health, family and environment, emotional experiences, outside relationships, your diet in detail, work, exercise, any shocks or memorable events in your life, and of course the major problems that first set you on the road to finding help. Together with all this the practitioner will note any previous medical diagnosis and any drugs which you might be taking. Relating all this in some detail will often cause you to link events that you may otherwise have thought were unconnected, and I often find patients experiencing illumination and self-education as they answer my questions. At the same time I am trying to form a picture from all the pieces of information. Very often I don't need to ask many questions; it all just comes tripping out and a pattern emerges as doors unlock. Having explored as much as one can verbally, the patient will be examined or touched in some way to form a bond and this is where the many trainings in diagnosis come into play. One of the most potent forms of diagnosis is the knowledge of corresponding feelings, thoughts and bodily patterns; that is why the mind, the body, the emotions and the spirit are all equally explored during the taking of the case history. All this information can be correlated to enable the treatment to be truly individual. Obviously, the more personal this approach is the better the healing will be: that is why three minutes in your GP's surgery is never enough time; yet it also explains why the same person may return to see their GP over and over again for the same problem.

Diagnosis

One of the best trainings in 'correlations' for diagnosis is framed by 'Ayurvedic Medicine', coined as the 'grandfather' of alternative medicine. The name itself means 'unimpeachable knowledge of the span or duration of life'. It is a traditional and very ancient Indian system of healing. The World Health Organisation emphasises the importance of its use. Its principles are truly 'whole-istic' and are the basis of much of what this book is about. Anyone wishing to know more about it should contact the Association of Ayurvedic Practitioners, 67 Tudor Court, North Wembley, Middlesex.

78

Conventional diagnosis is mainly concerned with isolable disease categories or 'agents' of disease, which it tries to name, change, control or destroy. The symptom is always uppermost in conventional medicine's diagnostic methods and after that comes the search for superficial 'mechanisms' causing the symptom; in other words, a precise cause for a specific disease. It is a frighteningly analytical approach and one that suffers through its isolation of all other factors. Instead of opening its horizons up, it shuts all doors as rapidly as possible in order to 'nail the victim' and name the problem. The Chinese have been using a completely different diagnostic system in their traditional medicine for thousands of years and it is to this kind of attitude that most natural healers are now turning. To them any information is important: the symptoms, the feelings, the smell of the patient, their colouring, their body temperature, their emotional state; in other words, a complete physiological and psychological pattern is observed. Every piece of information is gathered together and woven into a whole while great care is taken to examine the causes of two or more apparently unrelated symptoms. The Chinese call any disease a pattern of disharmony; they describe it as an imbalance in the body. To western doctors this oriental diagnostic approach is completely alien and unscientific, especially as in western medicine the question of cause and effect is quite secondary to the overall pattern. Very often, the Chinese would have six descriptions of a symptom whereas a western doctor would have awarded it one name.

All natural healing therapies are aimed at restoring harmony and balance of Yin and Yang (see page 12) to the body and individual, so a detailed diagnosis is important. Having said that, it should not be a frightening or untouchable subject and certainly good diagnosis takes years of experience. Yet, quite simply, if one is totally ignorant of such things, just to be able to understand the importance of keeping the body clean and well fed is diagnosis enough. Purifying the bloodstream and detoxifying the bowel requires no specific medical training, yet has saved many more lives than expensive X-ray machines, biopsies and blood tests.

Many diagnostic techniques are based on a knowledge of anatomy and physiology and one such technique is *reflexology*. It is also a healing technique and will be discussed in this light later on in this chapter. For diagnosis, it works on touching the feet at various points or reflexes. The degree of tenderness is noted and will give a very accurate reading to the trained practitioner if an organ or area is in a state of disorder. The same technique for using pressure points as a body reading is the basis of acupressure, and like reflexology this is a healing therapy in itself.

Another diagnostic technique is *iridology*, which involves health and personality diagnosis by examining the iris of the eye. This sort of analysis can often provide the fine tuning, hard to define by talking to and examination of the individual. Iridology does not name diseases, but aims to pinpoint information about a toxic condition in the body. Every part of your body relates to a section of the iris which can help ascertain problems and imbalances, while your nutritional pattern, your stress levels and your mental and emotional state record themselves in the iris. A faulty kidney or congested bowel can be noted and if this is done early in life, even genetic weaknesses can be helped and changed. Tiny details, veining and so on, are all taken into account, using a camera or magnifying lens.

Reading an eye is quite logical as the organs contained in the lower part of the body appear in the lower part of the eye, while the innermost organs like the stomach are shown in the centre of the eye near the pupil and the outermost organ, the skin, is shown on the periphery.

There are a great many methods of physical diagnosis and every practitioner has his or her own techniques. Some of those mentioned are ones that I use as needed, including diagnostic massage and 'Chinese pulse taking' which, like all good diagnosis, is based on touching the patient. The most important of all contact is considered in traditional Chinese medicine to be that of feeling the pulse. Compared with a western doctor's method of pulse-taking, it is like the difference between riding a bicycle and piloting a spacecraft. It is so significant that the Chinese often refer to 'going to have their pulse felt' rather than 'going to the doctor'. A very skilled practitioner of this art can determine both past and present medical history without verbal communication, although such a practitioner would also use this as well.

On the whole there are three major ingredients for good diagnosis: intuition, knowledge and experience. The ultimate aim of diagnosis should be to educate the patient in how to prevent the continuation of disease. In other words, it should not just be the practitioner who gains knowledge and experience — the patient should also share in the learning process.

The Treatment

Let me first make the comment that many practitioners achieve their results despite the methods of treatment they use. These are 'good' practitioners with a 'healing gift' which would be effective whatever they were doing to their patients. They have an overriding belief in their methods and they pass this enthusiasm on to their patients.

Getting better is what matters, not really how. There are many methods of treatment.

Firstly, of course, the individual's diet will be considered and alterations made. Usually everyone has something different recommended but in essence 'wholesome' food as described in Chapter 3 is the key. A fast may or may not be suggested as an initial step (see page 49). If the patient is taking any drugs, a replacement drug therapy is used to wean him or her off them slowly, replacing the drugs with herbs. At no time is the individual ever told to come off medication overnight; this would be as foolish as removing the crutches from a man with a broken leg before he showed signs of being able to walk a little. Depending on the drugs and the degree of dependence the patient has on them, this replacement may take weeks or even months. The process is always closely monitored and occasionally, if necessary, liaison with the patient's GP is maintained.

Just why are drugs so dangerous? Firstly, it must be said that powerful drugs extracted from herbs are good at dealing with certain symptoms; yet very often they create long-term problems and side effects more difficult to deal with — resulting so often in the use of more potent, powerful drugs! In the growing herb the concentration of drug-like substances is far less and it is buffered by softening agents and linked with other active ingredients, balancing the whole effect. With commercially produced drugs, the 'active ingredient' of the herb is isolated and used in a dangerously concentrated form. A typical and extremely well-known example of this is aspirin and its herb origin meadowsweet or willow. Aspirin is very potent and eventually destroys much of the stomach lining (and can cause ulcers), and by upsetting the stomach it in turn upsets the balance of the whole body, causing constipation, liver sluggishness and other disorders. Meadowsweet or willow is in fact just as effective in its natural state, if used as part of a natural healing treatment, yet it has none of the harmful side effects and has the bonus of many other healing properties beyond the salicylate acid or aspirin compound.

Antibiotics destroy the body's natural body defences and ability to fight bacteria. Even though they may initially 'cure' a symptom, their long term destructive elements are paramount. Antibiotics lower our natural reserves so much that very often a secondary infection or illness sets in immediately after the first as the body becomes suddenly 'unprotected'. Beyond all this, they destroy vital vitamins and minerals or inhibit their production in the body.

Non plant-based drugs, i.e. synthetic so-called copies, are even more hazardous in their effects and one only has to note the number of new drugs being taken off the market each month for proof of their dire effects. Sadly many of these drugs, banned and considered unsaleable in Britain, are sold cheaply to Third World countries (rather than being destroyed) and further evidence of their destructive qualities can be seen there.

Surgery

Through sheer horror at listening to so many stories about sections of the body being removed or cut into, I have now come to the conclusion that this is the most harmful side of conventional medicine, because once something is cut out, it cannot be replaced. When I hear about spleens and gall-bladders being removed supposedly to solve a problem, I am reminded of the 19th century clock jobbers or 'bodgers' as they were called. These clock workers were so ignorant that if a clock was not working because of a build-up of dirt, they would bend and twist the mechanism and even take out supposedly non-vital sections and throw them under the work bench. For a few months, the clock undoubtedly did function but soon more dirt collected and as the clock was missing its 'non-vital' parts, yet more problems arose. Later on the clock was often beyond all repair, even by a 'proper clocksmith' — whose first priority was always to clean the clock. In the same way the body builds up toxins because of blocked elimination channels, and this is the first thing that should be considered in any diagnosis.

So always make sure you understand exactly *why* surgery is being suggested — so very rarely is it vital.

HERBAL TREATMENT

We will be discussing the three major functions of herbs in the next chapter, but let us sub-divide them in a slightly different way to show the eight general therapy methods that a qualified practitioner might use. (Understanding the mechanisms of herbal formulations and the constituents and abilities of individual herbs takes time and training, so although the 'simples' and formulas I will be giving you can be safely used in preventing illness and toning the body, be careful to seek professional advice for more individual treatment.)

Herbs are used for:
1) *Stimulation:* To increase metabolic rate, drive, circulation, break up obstructions and warm the body. This sort of treatment should not be used in a very degenerated body.
2) *Blood Purification:* We will be discussing this in detail in Chapter 5, but generally speaking this sort of treatment can be applied to all disease categories.
3) *Tonification:* Important for degenerative diseases and severe acute diseases.

4) *Purging:* Used mostly for a very short period of time for those in generally good health with an acute illness, for the treatment of excessive toxic build-ups or for weak elimination. They must not be over-used as they deplete the body's energy levels.

5) *Tranquillisation:* There are three types — demulcents, nervines and anti-spasmodics. This therapy is often used towards the end of a treatment to sedate the patient for continued convalescence! Nervines calm tension generally and are often used before the treatment proper begins, while anti-spasmodics are useful for relaxing muscle spasms, making healing easier.

6) *Diuresis:* Often important to carry away toxins if the bowel is faulty. Intake of liquid and salt must be carefully regulated during this treatment.

7) *Emesis:* This category of herbs induces vomiting, useful if the contents of the stomach need to be emptied out quickly because of poor food combinations or nausea. They can also be used to counteract excessive build-ups in the stomach, but should not be used on weakened bodies. Using emetics in combination with mildly stimulating, soothing herbs reduces the amount of energy lost through the emesis.

8) *Sweating:* This is only used to treat diseases caused by external factors — colds, flu, fever, etc. There are two types — relaxing and stimulating — and they should not be used on already weakened bodies. It is particularly important not to use the stimulative kind.

The Herb and The Person

'Simple' treatment is something that anyone can practise for themselves (see p. 103), but most herbs and their dosage should be the province of the herbal practitioner and careful dosage is important due to the fact that some herbs have very powerful effects. Also the constitution of the user may be such that only weak herbs or weak combinations should be used. On the other hand, in the case of a person who has a generally strong and healthy constitution but is suffering from an acute ailment like a cold, cough or chicken pox, fairly strong herbs are used in smaller combinations. In other words, a more concentrated dose is required; time is of the essence, but the user should be able to withstand the force.

Acute Disease

This is considered to be mainly Yang in its nature i.e. it is hot and near the surface; so leaves, stalks and flowers are used with their lighter, more cooling make-up. However, rules like this are hard to make, as sometimes a disease can be neither acute nor chronic but something in-between i.e. a 'superficial' chronic ailment like non-persistent or 'occasional' migraine. Again, all individuals are treated as just that. Remember what I've said before, there is Yin in all Yang and Yang in all Yin.

The following is a typical treatment for an acute ailment.

Cough and Sore Throat Formula

3 parts Wild Cherry Bark 3 parts Coltsfoot Leaves 3 parts Comfrey Leaves	Primaries and Secondaries (i.e. the herbs of most vital importance)	This provides the 'force' of the formula.
1 part Elecampane Seed	Stimulant herb	This promotes the action of the other herbs.
1 part Lobelia Root	Antispasmodic herb	This reduces any bodily tension.
1 part Liquorice Root	Carminative or demulcent herb	This provides protection to the system (softening and coating) while making digestion and speed of absorption easier.

Just to expand a little on what those terms mean:
A *stimulant* herb increases functional activity and energy in the body; an *antispasmodic* is used to relieve nervous irritability and reduce or prevent excessive involuntary muscular contractions (spasms); a *carminative* herb contains a volatile oil that excites intestinal peristalsis and relieves and promotes the expulsion of gas or flatus from the gastro-intestinal tract; and a *demulcent* has mucilaginous properties that are soothing and protective internally to irritated and inflamed surfaces and tissues.

If possible, acute formulas should accompany gentle fasting, as this will speed the healing process.

The third kind of aproach to herbs is that used for chronic diseases.

Chronic Diseases

If you suffer from a chronic ailment such as colitis (ballooning of the colon wall), gall stones, arthritis or rheumatism, your body has

84

probably been weakened by the prolonged illness, and use of strong herbs in potent combinations would be far too drastic. Therefore, gentle herbs with a mild action should be used; although helping the particular area affected, they also raise the general vitality of the whole body. Eliminative herbs in particular must be used with great care and only gradual change should be sought. This is also true because these conditions are mainly Yin, cold and lacking in vitality and normal functioning abilities and are situated deep down inside the body. For this sort of treatment Yang herbs, mainly warming or 'hot' roots and barks, are used — dandelion root, ginger root, wild cherry bark, for example — as their action goes deep into the organs. As general body strength is regained then perhaps the formula can be altered using more forceful herbs with a more direct effect, but the situation must be carefully monitored, so that the arrival of the 'acute' stage can be recognised.

Here is a typical formula for treating a chronic complaint.

Ulcerative Colitis

2 *parts Alfalfa Leaves*   Nutritive and feeding herb, containing vitamins and minerals that build the system generally.
2 *parts Comfrey Root*   Nutritive, building, healing and coating.
1 *part Ginseng Root*   Safely stimulating, helpful in general weakness.
2 *parts Liquorice Root*   Antispasmodic and demulcent, i.e. relaxing, softening and coating, while making absorption of all other herbs easier and guiding them to the places most needed.
2 *parts Marshmallow Root*   Highly feeding and nutritious, softening, coating and antiseptic.
1 *part Dandelion Root*   Stimulating and gently detoxifying for major organs, mild yet safe in its action.
1 *part Ginger Root/1 part Cayenne Pod*   Warming, healing and antispasmodic, especially as chronic diseases are Yin and cold.

If the condition is greatly improved after a while on this formula then it would be altered, but chronic diseases need the most individual attention of all.

How Long will my Treatment take?

The point of explaining the composition of formulas and the various properties of the herbs used is to show the different approaches that will be made according to the individual problem. This of course has direct bearing on the length of time which the problem takes to heal. People are so frequently interested in how soon they will be better that I hope the breakdown will give some clue as to why some healing programmes cannot be hurried. Patience comes out of understanding and patience is needed. A general rule is to allow one month of treatment for every year an illness has lasted. So a chronic illness that has lasted twenty years may well take twenty months to cure. However, as the first few months are perhaps the most important in a healing programme, a short illness will probably take longer than the one month/one year ratio. I would give five months for a three year illness. Well after 'healing' has taken place, the healing therapies should continue to establish and assure the balance. Not to mention, of course, that a continued programme of correct eating and living must continue 'as part of life' to prevent further illness. Beyond this, if a healing programme is being blocked for psychological reasons no 'rule of thumb' can be applied. In other words the patient may subconsciously not wish to get better, thus extending the time of recovery, or preventing recovery altogether.

How Do I Take the Herbs?

The way in which the herbs are involved with the body depends on the particular problem. The major way we use herbs is by making them into herbal teas, but for obvious reasons only mild or pleasant flavours can form a herbal tea. This very often means, therefore, that bitter or strong tasting herbs are ground and made up into capsules with vegetable gelatine. The medicinal herb tea (rather than the herbal beverage which is not so strong and often sold in tea-bags) is one of the best ways of taking herbs as they go directly into the bloodstream, quickly to the stomach, making easy passage around the body. Not only this, but it makes coming off tea and coffee a natural event with an immediate substitute. On the whole, most tea infusions are made up of flowers, stalks and leaves but occasionally barks and roots. The former need only an *infusion* to gain their healing powers while to extract the qualities from barks and roots needs a longer steeping called a *decoction*. Very often the two are made separately and then combined.

Making a Herbal Tea — Infusion and Decoction

This need not be the chore that one might at first imagine; after all it is no more complicated than making a pot of Indian tea. Warm the pot, use one ounce of herb to one pint of boiling water and allow to infuse for from ten to twenty minutes. Drink teas with honey or fructose if you like a sweet taste. If a decoction is needed then simmer the herbs in water, just covering them for about an hour in a pot. Once strained, they can be drunk as they are or added to the infusion. Your practitioner will guide you as to just what to do.

If you go out to work, you can take herbal tea with you in a flask, and it is important to do so as you should drink at least three cups a day on a normal healing programme. Making the tea weaker and drinking it more frequently is permissible and in many ways more effective.

Herbs in Capsules

You are generally given the capsules and powdered herbs separately, and it is an easy and pleasant job to fill them. If your hands are not capable of fiddly work, get someone to help you. Making your own pills like this avoids the cost and detrimental effects of commercial buffers, mordants and fixatives, while involving you more fully in your own healing. However some herbal pills are made using natural buffers and fixatives. Some herbs are weakened by these additives, but in other cases they provide a necessary softening action.

Herbal Tinctures

These are highly concentrated herbal extracts, preserved in alcohol or occasionally apple cider vinegar (for children especially). They are useful if the herb is unpalatable or if it needs to be administered into the ear or eye as drops. Also some herbs are so strong that their qualities are not easily extracted by water, needing the strength of the alcohol. Sometimes also, if someone with a chronic problem will not continue taking as much herbal tea as they should over a long period of time, this is the next best answer; directions will always be on the bottle.

Herbal Linaments

Herbal extracts made with apple cider vinegar or alcohol and often diluted 50% with distilled water. They are rubbed on to the skin for treating strains and sprains and also for some inflamed arthritic conditions, bringing relaxing warmth to the area.

Herbal Syrups

These are most useful for things like coughs and some sore throats as they 'coat' and soften the areas they come in contact with. They are made as a decoction and have honey or glycerine added to provide the syrup effect.

Herbal Salves or Ointments

Most obviously used in conjunction with skin problems, these generally accompany a herbal tea designed to treat such a complaint. They are made with herbs, beeswax and olive oil.

Herbal Fomentations or Compresses

These are external applications of herbs made from a herb tea and applied with a muslin cloth dipped in it. Very often strong herbs are used which should not be taken orally. They are used to treat minor ailments, swellings, pains, colds etc. Specific instructions would always be given as heat without burning is important. Compresses often bring almost instant relief.

Herbal Poultices or Plasters

A poultice is made from macerated or powdered herbs (slightly moistened with warm water if powdered) and applied directly to the skin via the cloth. They are very useful for inflammation, blood poisoning, skin eruptions etc. and generally help with a more speedy healing of the area.

Herbal Water Therapy

Herbs placed in a bowl of boiling water and allowed to cool down to skin temperature can then be used as foot or hand baths, allowing herbs to enter the body gently via osmotic pressure. This is very useful for circulatory problems or skin disorders.

ADDITIONAL TREATMENT

Although herbal medicine stands up as a major healing therapy on its own, like all forms of natural healing, it has links with other treatments; different ones appropriate to differing problems. We have already discussed in brief some of the many diagnostic methods and at the time, I mentioned that some of them were not only used for diagnosis, but also for the actual healing treatment. It is quite likely that your herbal practitioner will suggest some other help, either administering it personally or directing you to a specialist in that particular form of healing.

Probably the most frequent forms of joint healing methods I use are *massage* and subsequently *chiropractic* or *osteopathic* skills, and, to a certain extent, acupuncture. During the massage, faults in the spine are often noted and these lead to the two latter practitioners. You see what a 'chain' natural healing is. Only arrogance on the part of the practitioner stops this chain at the cost of the patient — which in turn reflects badly on the reputation of the practitioner!

Massage

This can take so many forms, from just gentle relaxing of the body to deep tissue massage, acupressure massage or lymphatic draining. But what any massage will do for you is help to balance imbalances of all organs and systems, acting through the skin and nerves. Circulation is improved and tensions removed, if nothing else, and I always find that a massaged body is far more receptive to herbs than a tense, 'untouched' one. Even inexperienced hands can do something to relieve tensions held in the neck (although the spine should never be touched) but a good, well qualified masseuse is always the best. Acupressure massage will activate certain points in the body so that the body's own healing forces are put into action. This is a bit like knowing how to plug into the mains electricity and is as potent. All these natural forces are always present but few know how to initiate them.

The Spine

This is a most important part of the body and seeing that it is properly aligned with the hips sitting naturally is vital. Many problems can be caused by wrong spine alignment. Apart from the more obvious ones other problems include menstrual malfunction or severe headaches. Many spines have been out of line for years from some kind of an accident — or even from birth!

Note: never massage the spine.

Reflexology

This is often treated as part of a massage as it involves 'massaging the reflexes of the feet'. These stimulate healing forces latent in the body affecting all systems and organs. Tensions are relaxed, normal energy flow is renewed and all aspects are generally rejuvenated, greatly aiding the 'whole' healing approach to the body.

Acupuncture

Scoffed at until fairly recently by western medicine as unscientific, it has been used in China, Japan and other eastern countries hand in hand with herbalism for thousands of years. Interestingly enough it is now sometimes available on the NHS. Occasionally some people are apprehensive at the thought of having needles stuck into them, but believe me it doesn't hurt and they are by no means the long 'syringe' type needles that most of us have experienced for vaccination since babyhood. They are delicate 'pin-pricking' slithers of gold or silver. However, if you really dislike the idea, then try acupressure massage and experience the healing points that way. Again always choose a well-qualified acupuncturist (it takes many years of training), as haphazard sticking in of needles can lead to further complications. There are even seven points on the body where the accidental sticking in of needles can be fatal. Certain cases of GPs going on five day crash courses have done untold harm to their patients, so avoid any offers in that direction. The best acupuncturists I know have a long training in China.

Needles are placed at precise points (although all are placed according to the individual's needs) and the pattern of where to place them follows ancient instructions based on thousands of years of empirical knowledge. Part of what the acupuncture needle does is encourage the production of endorphins in the brain, making you feel envigorated yet calm, producing a generally healing effect on mind and body. They re-balance bodily energies through the whole body and can do so quite rapidly (i.e. within half an hour) along the meridians or healing lines throughout the body. Initially just a body balance is generally given, with more specific treatment coming in a further session. Again, as with the herbs, this all takes time.

There are many other additional therapies and treatments but I have listed the major ones that I find most useful and have had practical experience of. Just as every patient is an individual, so is every practitioner and his/her approaches will differ accordingly. But there is one more treatment that I haven't mentioned which I consider of prime importance.

Water Therapy

I have kept it apart from the others as it can so easily be practised by anybody and essentially in the home. Just being in a tub of very hot water releasing tensions, aches and pains (the Japanese are very fond of this) is one of the easiest ways of healing ourselves I know. Adding some relaxant herbs like hops, lemon balm or vervain with some Epsom Salts, further enhances this experience. A one minute brisk cold shower is essential after this, to close opened pores and stimulate the circulation.

At this point we are back to many of the aspects in Chapter 2, as self-healing by massaging your feet, massaging your partner's neck or whatever is just as important as having professional help — and it's free!

A Reminder

With all or some of these healing treatments, plus a revised diet being put into action, changes are bound to arise in the body. I have mentioned the 'healing crisis' and will explain more about it in the next chapter, but I would just like to remind you again of its existence. Do let me remind you also that young, healthy bodies with an acute illness can easily withstand a healing crisis, but a chronically sick, debilitated body has to be treated much more gently. Yet both should be guided by an experienced practitioner (an unguided healing crisis of a chronic disease can occasionally become a death crisis, which speaks for itself).

To close this chapter, here is the story of another patient of mine, Mr Balaam of Stowlangtowf in Suffolk. The recounting of healing experience is part of any natural healing process. Sharing with other sufferers is a vital and important process. I have found that the vast majority of people who seek help have done so due to the encouragement and enthusiasm for such methods from those who have already received benefit. This is a very striking difference between natural healing and conventional medicine in that the processes of natural healing are totally dependent upon the conscious and willing participation of the person being treated with the practitioner playing the role of teacher. (That is not to say that the practitioner judiciously selects only patients he thinks will get better.) This leads towards the patients themselves becoming not only well informed about the methods that bring about their recovery, but also enabling them to point out to others how they could make positive progress themselves. In conventional treatment, more often than not the patient has a totally passive role, only vaguely understanding the processes involved in the treatment. This makes it impossible for them to recommend a treatment to a friend, as they only really appreciate irrelevant aspects of it.

For the information of readers I am now 64 years old. I served in the army from before World War II until December 1949, I then joined the police force and was a country policeman (cycling and walking the old fashioned way) and retired after 25 years service enjoying every minute. I then worked as a highways inspector for the county council. Now I have taken early retirement.

After at least 25 years of spinal pain which was attributed to slipped discs and other disc damage, neck and shoulder pains caused by arthritis, I decided after hearing a local radio broadcast, to visit Jill Davies at the Thornham Herb Garden. I have always been very sceptical about any so-called 'way out' treatments, but there comes a time when enough is enough, so I went. I must say here that about nine years ago I had an operation at a hospital in Cambridge to remove and repair the bottom four spinal discs and remove a nerve in the leg. This course was recommended as I was losing the use of my left leg and suffering very severe pains. The

91

operation 'appeared' at the time to be a success as I was without pain for about three months, then gradually the pains started again as before. On top of this I was having treatment for high blood pressure and angina.

Jill, having noted all this, must have thought as I did, that it was a hopeless case — but not at all. My wife (who attended the consultation with me) and I were rather taken aback at the suggestions and obvious care given to my individual case. I had a feeling that here was someone who could do something for me.

I started at once to take the herbal teas and herbal powders and changed my ways of eating as suggested and believe me I could feel after a few days something was happening. This may sound almost unreal, but believe me it is true. I suddenly felt that I had no need to take painkilling tablets or medicine (at this time — November 1983 — I was getting very worried as to the amount of painkilling medication I was having to take). It is now April '84 and I have no need or desire to resort to painkillers, in fact, I came off them many months ago. This has all been reported to my doctor (a very good and understanding one), he seems quite happy although a bit sceptical. I am still taking medicine from him for the angina but have stopped the pills for water retention as well as the painkillers. My blood pressure has been normal and I have had no angina symptoms (previously present even when I was on the doctor's drugs) since starting the herbal treatment, in fact, I feel quite fit and well.

I still get lower back pain if I subject it to severe stress i.e. heavy or prolonged gardening or lifting, but of course normal people get this as well. At least now it doesn't persist on and on; we must also remember we are trying to cure something that has been over 25 years getting to this stage. But! It is working!

You must not be alarmed when you hear the no's, it is the multitude of yes's that make it exciting! Take it from me it is worthwhile and not as 'way out' as you may think. The herbal teas are delicious and much more refreshing than ordinary tea. They have none of the acid content of normal tea, and you get the feeling they are doing you much more good.

I was also advised by Jill to have acupressure massage and some spine alignment in conjunction with the herbal treatment and with these two treatments, I feel a different person. With a little effort, faith and trust I can recommend herbal treatment to anyone. I know it works.

CHAPTER FIVE

The Simplicity of Disease

EASY UNDERSTANDING OF THE CAUSES OF ILLNESS, ITS PATH AND CURE

On the whole disease is viewed as an invasive mystery, something that 'just happens' and must be treated 'from the outside'. Actually, the body has a highly complex and amazing system of coping with its own problems. For instance, damaged skin provokes a response from the circulatory system — inflammation, redness, swelling — which is totally healthy and most important for the protection of the area. The local blood vessels break down, flushing the affected area with blood and allowing the white blood cells — the body's 'policemen' — to consume any dead or damaged cells or bacteria. When this cleansing process has been completed, the swelling will go down of its own accord. But normally our first reaction is to reduce the swelling, not realising that this is hindering the body in healing itself! Similarly, we try to reduce a fever, but the body raises our temperature to stop the spread of the disease: mucoid lymph is thinned, thus improving our 'auto-immune' system. Yet we would not need this bodily reaction if the body was clean and healthy.

Disease germs, like flies, are all around us, and like all scavengers, they are only interested in, or able to live on, weak, impaired cells where dirt, mucus and toxins are present. In other words, we do not 'catch' germs, they infest a dirty body just like a dirty dustbin. A high temperature is indeed one of the body's defence mechanisms, but it is also a signal that should not be ignored or suppressed as it tells us that 'all is not well'. Either the body is toxic and is for some reason unable to 'dump' its rubbish, which means attention must be paid to the bowel and other elimination channels; or it is deficient in some vital need — for example a teething baby might be lacking in calcium, so organic calcium would bring the temperature back to normal. Generally speaking, the rest of the body must supply the needs of the affected areas, and in a strong, healthy body the necessary resources are available. And even a weak body can be remarkably robust. Life maintenance, in other words, at all times and all cost is the body's primary concern. So just remember this and bear in mind that all forms of natural healing are only concerned with assisting these natural bodily reactions.

The major area in which we defend the body against disease seems to be the digestive system, where there are large concentrations of lymphatic tissue with white blood cells at the ready. Again, the body has thought it all out for us, it knows that this is the first stop for all noxious toxic substances and sensibly places its policemen there. Added to this is the presence of extremely potent hydrochloric acid and its enzyme henchman pepsin, whose job is to break down protein. Anything that escapes this is attacked later on by pancreatic juices and anything that slips through this net meets its doom with the vicious advances of the liver. It is interesting to note, therefore, that enteric diseases, epidemics, plagues, etc, are all based on a widespread lack of acid in the stomach. Such diseases are often the bane of the Third World, yet it is the very foods which help to produce these digestive acids that originate mainly from those parts of the world. Hot spices increase the secretion of stomach juices and are indeed vital in hot 'fermentative and putrefactive' climates — and generally helpful as a preventive measure against disease in the west, too.

But western diet and stress levels tend to produce excess acid — hyperacidity — which brings us back to the question of 'balance of all throughout'. If we treat our digestive system properly it will always look after us! Let us now look at the digestive system in more detail and consider how the vital organs can be kept strong and healthy.

When food is swallowed, digestive enzymes attack it and it is gradually released from the stomach into the duodenum. Here it mixes with bile from the liver and gall bladder used for the digestion of fats, plus enzymes and alkalis from the pancreas. Many 'good bits' are absorbed through the wall of the small intestine at this point. The food goes on into the large intestine where water and nutrients are absorbed — extracting these from the waste material is an important job here. As the large intestine or colon is at the end of the digestive process, its job is to deal with all that remains of whatever we have swallowed. Nutrients and toxins are exchanged through the colon wall, so the colon can be considered both eliminative and absorptive.

Anything toxic that is left at this stage must be eliminated from the body — and all food and drink inevitably produces toxic waste.

There are five major elimination channels:

The bowel, for passing bulky waste — faeces (the major elimination channel)
The kidneys and urinary system, for passing watery waste — urine
The skin, for releasing watery excesses — sweat (also the largest organ and greatest surface area for elimination)
The lungs, for eliminating sticky build-ups — mucus
The lymphatic system, for discharging lymph full of toxins from the blood stream.

All the major channels are interrelated and if one is blocked or semi-blocked for any reason, one of the others will try to take over its job. But the major channel is the bowel and if this becomes blocked it causes a chain reaction of problems throughout the body. If the bowels are congested and sluggish, this puts pressure on the liver, whose job it is to convert food, store and release nutrients and destroy, neutralise or dilute poisons and toxins. Sometimes the liver becomes overworked through sheer volume of food toxins, and can be further strained by having to cope with synthetic hormones, antibiotics or the like. This failure of the liver throws more responsibility back on the lymphatic system; if this fails, cysts, malignancy or inflammation of the glands can occur. The next along in the chain could be the kidneys and urinary system, followed by the skin. Shedding toxins through the skin results in body odour, rashes, greasy skin and so on. As a last resort, the body might use the nose and lungs to discharge mucus, causing colds, coughs or even pneumonia. The order of the chain differs from individual to individual, but all this is because the bowel could not function properly!

It is impossible to overstate the importance of keeping the bowel in good working order. Having the digestive system and elimination channels in good condition is like having a well-tuned car — it will

use less fuel and you will get better mileage and higher performance!
See page 157 for the names of other books which will tell you more about this.

THE BOWEL

Some Causes of Bowel Congestion

Inherent weakness: passed down by generations.

Mucus-forming foods: flours, pastries, cakes, milk, cheese, processed foods in general. The sticky mucus adheres to the walls of the intestine like wallpaper, layer upon layer. This thickens the intestine allowing less room for faecal matter to pass through.

Sedentary occupations: if you get plenty of exercise, the increased activity of the diaphragm and abdominal muscles supports the intestine in its true position, thus making the movement and working of the large intestine easier.

Bad posture: stooping or 'slouching' weakens the abdominal muscles and causes congestion of the liver and all other abdominal organs. These also become over-filled with blood, which coupled with a lack of support from the abdominal muscles can cause prolapse. The result is that the bowel becomes distended and may even become infected. Erect posture ensures correct breathing, blood circulation and muscle tone.

Over-consumption of liquid foods: porridges, soups and gruels initially provide 'bulk', yet soon break down to a lot of water causing constipation.

Lack of roughage and mucilaginous foods which aid peristaltic movement.

Ignoring the bowel: putting off going to the toilet because you are too busy or should be leaving for work or whatever, is a classic reason for constipation. Delays mean constipation and putrefaction.

Mental stress can produce bowel tension, which results in spasms and causes pain and distention. This may lead to colitis (ballooning of the colon), but at best causes constipation and/or diarrhoea.

Some of the Results of Bowel Misuse

If the colon wall is thickened by ancient mucus, faecal matter has to squeeze its way through, stagnating and constipating as it does so.

96

At worst, the faeces need to become watery in order to pass through, which means that diarrhoea can be a sign of severe constipation.

Mucus congestion also stops the free flow of nutrients to and from the rest of the body. Intestinal clogging can mean that the body absorbs as little as ten per cent of the nutrients in the food eaten. This means that you tend to eat more and more to take in the energy you need — and becoming overweight is the most obvious result.

Layers of mucus are heavy and the bowel, weakening under the strain, loses its elasticity and balloons out. These can lead to a range of ailments from colitis to a prolapsed bowel. Ballooning can also occur if the bowel is trying to cope with 'backed up', uneliminated faeces.

Strictures, narrowing of the passages due to tissue damage which can follow colitis; ulceration, a common result of chronic auto-intoxication and constipation; and adhesions, resulting from breakdown of tissue and mucus membranes, are yet more unpleasant consequences of allowing the bowel to clog up.

If you suffer from any of the following symptoms, a faulty bowel may be to blame: low energy levels, swollen lymph glands, headaches, liver diseases (hepatitis, jaundice), nausea, kidney congestion, backache, loss of appetite, psoriasis, bad breath, appendicitis, acne — the list is endless.

It may surprise you to learn that three bowel movements a day — roughly one after each meal, with the major one being after breakfast — should be the norm. Only one bowel movement a day can mean that the food from several meals can be in the colon at any one time, some body wastes being retained for fifty hours or more. The longer the faeces remain in the body, the more compact and solid the stool will be. Ideally, bowel movements should be bulky but not pressed or very formed and mid-brown in colour. There is a great deal of difference between this and diarrhoea. Only Yogis could manage one bowel movement a day; for most of us two should be a bare minimum. A long urination after a bowel movement signals the complete emptying of the bowel.

Correct eating habits as outlined in Chapter 3, starting with Dr Christopher's three-day cleanse (see page 50) will do much to keep the bowel healthy. Here are a few tonics that will help regularise or rebuild a weakened bowel.

Note: On the whole, leaves and flowers are used in making herbal teas, but occasionally roots are used, particularly for chronic conditions (see decoctions p. 86). A skilled practitioner will, of course, use knowledge and intuition.

Dr Christopher's Lower Bowel Tonic

This formula is pleasant tasting and its gentle construction is ideal for regularising a constipated bowel. It does not act as a laxative, yet tones, builds, re-strengthens and removes old mucus layer by layer (often there are pounds of ancient mucus to remove). More than anything else, this formula will only encourage peristaltic movement by the body itself, rather than forcing it to work and leaving it weakened afterwards. (See Dr Christopher's book 'Childhood Diseases' and the programmes advised as part of this formula.)

> 1 part Turkey Root Rhubarb
> 1 part Barberry Bark
> 1 part Cascara Sagrada Bark
> 1 part Cayenne
> 1 part Ginger
> 1 part Golden Seal Root
> 1 part Lobelia
> 1 part Red Raspberry Leaves
> 1 part Fennel

Powder and place in vegetable gelatine capsules. Take two capsules at mealtimes, three times daily; or to suit your own needs, anything from one to fifteen a day is allowable.

N.B. Omit the Golden Seal after two months and replace with thyme. Golden Seal destroys B vitamins if taken long-term. This formula should not be taken for longer than one year.

Bowel Building Tea

This tea is a good addition to the Bowel Formula above.

3 parts Ginger   Wonderful stimulant to the whole system and helps 'activate' the other herbs. Excellent for relieving and correcting cramps, pains and flatulence.

1 part Dill   Tasty and excellent for flatulence.

1 part Fennel   Helpful for flatulence, indigestion, cramps, spasms, pinworms and general liver malfunctions.

1 part Sage   A laxative, very helpful for flatulence also.

1 part Cayenne   Slightly laxative, it stimulates the organs it passes through, cleansing and rebuilding as it goes. Helpful in the removal of mucus.

2 parts Liquorice (shredded)   A mild laxative, it is also a detoxifier.

2 parts Elderflower   A gentle laxative and aperient, detoxifying the bowel and other eliminative channels, removing mucus etc.

1 part Red Raspberry Leaves   This herb is an astringent, acting on the internal tissues and membranes, due to its citrate of iron content and blood-making, regulating properties.

1 part Comfrey   As a cell-proliferant, this will rebuild the walls of the bowel and intestine, its mucilaginous qualities protecting the bowel from the harsh effects of food fibre during the rebuilding process.

1 part Marigold   An emollient which relieves pain from cell deterioration in chronic bowel conditions. Otherwise it is generally healing and restorative of all it comes in contact with. Comfrey and marigold work well together. Helpful for piles, fissures, etc.

1 part Blackthorn Flowers (Prunus spinosa)   Safe and gentle purgative.

Use one ounce of this mixture per pint of water.

Bowel Sweets

A sweet-tasting alternative to the above, ideal for children.

1 part chopped Raisins or Figs   1 part powdered Flaxseed
1 part Powdered Root of Liquorice   (Linseed)
                                                   1 part Powdered Arrowroot

Mix together with enough blackstrap molasses and honey to mould into small balls; coat with shredded coconut so the little balls will not be sticky to touch. Chill in the fridge and serve on demand!

Diarrhoea Tea

A stronger formula for chronic constipation.

1 part Mullein   Its mucilaginous qualities help to coat and protect the bowel. It is also antispasmodic to help with any associated pain.

3 parts Marshmallow   The mucilage in this herb is protective and healing of the irritations caused by the diarrhoea.

1 part Plantain   This cooling, soothing herb greatly helps diarrhoea.

1 part Nettles   Iron content counteracts anaemia which can cause diarrhoea.

1 part Yellow Dock   Has similar properties to nettles.

3 parts Oak Bark   Astringent and tightening, it helps strengthen.

1 part Wood Betony   Alterative and nervine, it is wonderful for diarrhoea.

1 part Camomile   Binding, calming and soothing.

2 parts Motherwort   Tonic to gastro-intestinal tract helpful for debilitation or weakness with diarrhoea.

1 part Comfrey   Its cell-proliferant qualities repair any damaged tissue.

Note: Gerard House do a 'Fenulin Tablet' for *non-persistant* diarrhoea.

Regulariser

This is a very safe and effective recipe for very debilitated bowel conditions.

1 part Flaxseed (Linseed)
1 part Psyllium Seed (the seed of plantain)
1 part Liquorice Powder Root
1 part whole Raisins

Soak 2 tablespoons of mix overnight in a cup of boiling water. In the morning it will have expanded. Sieve and keep the liquid. Take three tablespoons at a time each hour if necessary.

Laxative Gruel

This is a recipe of Dr Christopher's, again for very debilitated bowel conditions.

3 parts Flaxseed   gives bulk
3 parts Psyllium Seed   gives bulk
3 parts Liquorice Root   an aperient or very mild laxative
3 parts Marshmallow Root   assists clearance of hard stools
3 parts Comfrey Root   healing and rebuilding in weakened bowel areas; also provides lubrication
1 part Lobelia   accentuates and directs herbs

As a complete alternative for constipation, the two combinations given below are pre-made up on a commercial basis:

Natural Flow sell psyllium seed capsules which are useful for emergencies, and 'Kalenite Herbal Blend' tablets based on Robert Gray's formula or their own 'Colonite' tablets, which are excellent for those who have had long-term bowel problems. They aid cleansing of hardened mucus and other toxic material from the colon, being composed of acacia gum, cloves, butternut bark, blessed thistle, plantain, red clover, corn silk extract and yellow dock root.

Gerard House produce 'fenulin' tablets or powder, ideal for general bowel weakness, colitis, diarrhoea or diviticulitis — this formula is made up of fenugreek, turkey rhubarb, slippery elm, bayberry and golden seal.

100

For Chronic Diarrhoea or Dysentery

Astringent herbs should be taken for immediate help — make a tisane from equal parts of raspberry leaves and marshmallow leaves (both astringent) and blackberry root (mucilaginous). This combination is tightening and toning, yet softening and coating.

Food

The whole grain flask porridge (see page 37) with prunes is an ideal breakfast for those with bowel complaints. Do not be tempted to eat 'wheat bran', as its coarse effect on a weakened bowel can lead to even greater problems. 'Whole grain' contains the softer and weaker elements that nature intended, and should always be eaten in preference to bran, which leeches minerals from the body. As an aid to regularity, add a small amount of psyllium seed and flax seed (available from the Suffolk Spice and Herb Company under the name of 'Whole Grain Regulariser').

If you are suffering from a severe bowel problem — prolapse, ulceration, diviticulitis, colitis — always seek the help of a practitioner. You must keep to gentle foods — pureed, liquidised or finely chopped — while the healing process is going on. A tip-u-up chair is often helpful in the case of a prolapse, as it can help to realign the intestines. Never use an enema for these chronic conditions — they can be vital in treating some acute diseases, but always seek professional help.

Supplements

Increase intake of B vitamins, wheatgerm and brewers' yeast. Take acidophilus or Prima-dophilus (available from Natural Flow) to repopulate the flora of the colon and produce necessary 'energy' for easy peristalsis.

Eat vegetables rich in potassium and magnesium (for all this eat plenty of sprouted seeds and beans).

Other Treatments

Massage of the abdomen is helpful. Use castor oil (or even a castor oil pack — again, seek professional advice on this) and make massaging movements with your hands. Start on the right hand bottom side and move upwards, along and down to follow the shape of the colon. Repeat several times, keeping your hands in contact with the skin at all times. Skin brushing is another vital aid to elimination of mucus via stimulation of the lymphatic system.

The Psychological Approach

Bowel problems are often linked with lung problems — and vice versa — and in the 'emotion' category this represents anguish, anxiousness and a tendency to be unwilling to let go — of money, people, other emotions or whatever. Just learning to accept, enjoy and be generous in every aspect of your life will help any bowel conditions.

THE MULTI-TALENTS OF HERBS

We have covered in detail the major elimination channel of the bowel and how to 'manage' it. Promoting proper elimination is one of the major attributes of herbs. So before going any further let us stop and examine the three major functions of herbs:

1) Eliminate and Detoxify

By using:

a) *Laxative herbs* — these promote bowel movements to a greater or lesser extent. Most are used to encourage the bowel to work for itself.

b) *Blood purifiers* — one of the most important sorts of herbs, as any blood purification and neutralisation of excess acidity will heal most diseases. They remove excess moisture, dispel heat, stimulate defence mechanisms and provide a strong alkaline effect, removing mucus, cholesterol, plaque and other toxins.

c) *Diuretics* — these control fluid balance and as the body consists mostly of water, this is vital. Water imbalances are quick to occur and our emotions are directly connected to this. Water retention easily leads to depression and weakness, particularly in the case of pre-menstrual tension. Generally diuretics increase the flow of urine and are often combined with a 'demulcent' herb to soften their action.

d) *Diaphoretics* — these herbs induce sweating and work best on an empty bowel and stomach — but don't use laxatives to empty them. There are two types; 'relaxing' and 'stimulating' — used respectively for chronic and acute diseases.

During elimination and detoxification the body will become weak and lacking in energy and therefore you need also to:

2) Support and Maintain

Certain herbs counteract physical symptoms in a positive way. They allow the body to heal itself. They are specifically useful in degenerative or chronic disease; or severe acute diseases.

They carry the body for a while by using:

a) *Analgesics* — pain relief herbs; pain exacerbates any illness so help with this is vital.

b) *Anti-asthmatics* — they relieve the symptoms of asthma and help break up mucus enabling the healing process to go ahead.

c) *Anti-acids* — they neutralise excess acids in the stomach and intestines and often have demulcent properties.

d) *Demulcents* — these soothe, coat and heal, protecting the organ or tissue until healing has taken place.

e) *Anti-catarrhals* — counteract the formation of mucus, providing a 'rest' for the body.

f) *Anti-pyretics* — cooling herbs that reduce or prevent fevers, allowing mending of the system.

g) *Antiseptics* — they prevent the growth of bacteria.

There are many more such 'supportive and maintaining' categories, but these are the most important ones.

And once the body is on its way back to health, it is important, finally, to:

3) Build and Tone

Tonics are vital for providing energy for the organs so they can rebuild and work more efficiently. They should always be used during an acute disease, while they are also important for building energy in those depleted from a chronic illness. Tonics nourish and feed the organs while affecting the whole body and particularly all systems. They can be subdivided as follows:

a) *Nerve tonics* — they calm nervous tension and nourish the nervous system.

b) *Cardiac or heart tonics* — nourish, feed and tune the heart.

c) *Stomach tonics and bitters* — activate the digestive juices, and provide minerals, vitamins and nutrients.

d) *Liver tonics or 'Hepatics'* — use mostly bitter herbs to stimulate and build.

e) *Biliary tonics* — these stimulate bile.

f) *Sexual tonics* — these aid sexual function.

SIMPLES

The easiest and safest form of self-help treatment for the layman is the use of mild, 'safe' herbs with general healing properties which, used over a long period of time, will help the specific ailment as a result of the overall beneficial effect on the whole body. For additional benefit to a certain part of the body, specific herbs should be used, and I shall be coming to that in a moment. This form of natural medicine is called 'simpling' and is particularly effective if you can use herbs grown in your own garden or at least locally and organically. Here are some suggestions for 'simples' that can have specific application to certain organs or systems.

For the Kidneys and Urinary System

Dandelion (Taraxacum officinale): grows wild and is common all over Britain. The safest of all the diuretics in the plant kingdom, it can be taken long-term with nothing but beneficial building effects,

The ribbed fruit is scaly towards the top; it has a parachute of white hairs at the end of a long stem (×2)

on one side of the florets the petal extends to form a five-toothed strap (×2)

Dandelion

strengthening and conditioning the kidneys. It is helpful for water retention due to its high potassium content. It is very rich in most minerals.

Marshmallow (Althaea officinalis): grows wild and is reasonably common in marshy or watery areas of Britain. A gentle, safe, mucilaginous diuretic, it is a good partner to dandelion for the severest of urinary problems.

Marshmallow

For the Skin

Yarrow (Achillea millefolium): grows wild and is common all over Britain. Although bitter-tasting it is very safe and useful. It prevents watery secretions of an excessive nature from invading the rest of the body and instead it channels them to the skin, producing perspiration — and shedding of toxins. It also regulates the activity of the sebaceous glands found in the upper layers of the skin.

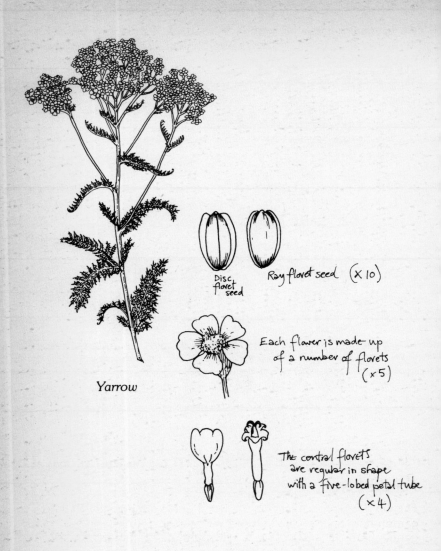

Disc floret seed

Ray floret seed (X 10)

Each flower is made up of a number of florets (x 5)

The central florets are regular in shape with a five-lobed petal tube (x 4)

Yarrow

Chickweed (Stellaria media): grows wild and is common all over Britain — a common garden herb. An ancient and safe herb, it not only produces excellent skin elimination via perspiration, but it also helps clear the colon of mucus and putrefying material. Very cooling to the blood and excellent in salads!

Chickweed

For the Lungs

Hyssop (Hyssopus officinalis): native to Europe, it is a very common garden herb and is starting to occur naturally in Britain. A safe and gentle herb, it is effective for all pulmonary complaints as an expectorant and tonic and to induce sweating. It helps to relieve all lung/respiratory congestions, partly due to its volatile oils.

Mullein (Verbascum thapsus): reasonably common, growing wild throughout Britain. Anti-asthmatic, anti-catarrhal, it is truly a lung all-rounder. Its softening, feeding and safe yet slightly narcotic properties make it an excellent painkiller, ideal for asthmatics. It helps to absorb accumulations of mucus and other toxins.

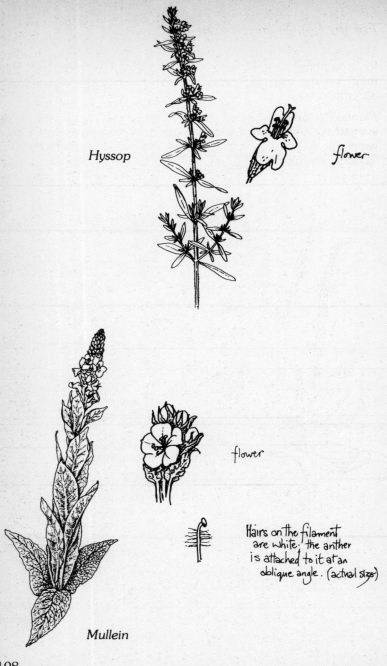

Hyssop

flower

flower

Hairs on the filament
are white. the anther
is attached to it at an
oblique angle. (actual size)

Mullein

For the Lymphatic System

Mullein (Verbasum thapsus): chosen again, I know, but it is excellent for promoting the absorption of the fluids which have escaped from their vessels through rupturing. It also absorbs any morbid accumulations.

Plantain (Plantago major): found in all gardens and wild almost everywhere. A common and wayside herb, it generally 'heals' the lymphatic system, absorbing poisons and reducing swellings. It is a 'cooling' alterative.

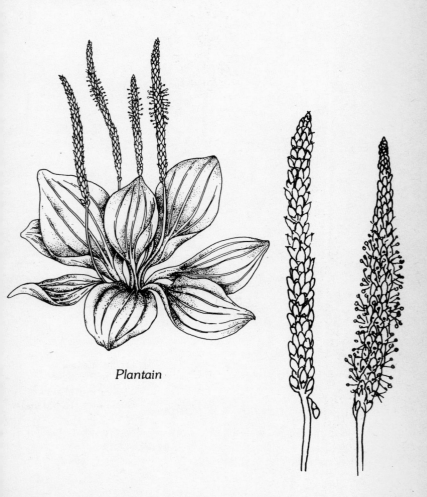

Plantain

For the Liver

Dandelion (Taraxacum officinale): ideal for the kidneys (see page 104), it is also one of the best hepatic herbs due to its mineral content. It improves digestion, influences the liver generally and stimulates secretion of bile while also breaking down gall-stones.

Agrimony (Agrimonia eupatoria): like dandelion, it is a common British weed and excellent for all liver complaints, especially jaundice. It gives tone to the entire system and promotes the assimilation of food. It is an astringent.

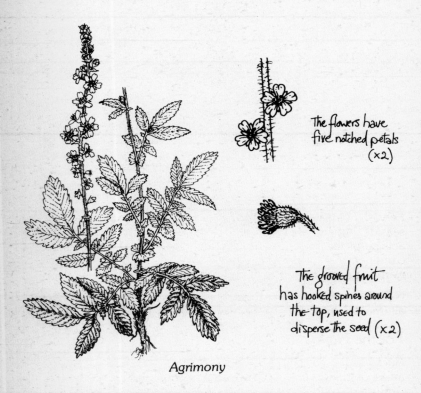

The flowers have five notched petals (x2)

The grooved fruit has hooked spines around the top, used to disperse the seed (x2)

Agrimony

For the Spleen, Stomach and Pancreas

Lemon Balm (Melissa officinalis): common wayside and garden herb. Valuable aid in digestion and activation of the spleen, it is helpful when nausea and vomiting occur.

110

Lemon Balm

Fennel (Foeniculum vulgare): very common wild, especially near the seaside, but also frequent in gardens. As a stomachic, it excites the activity of the stomach and activates, therefore, the spleen; it is a carminative and helpful for indigestion, partly due to its aromatic/ warming qualities.

N.B. If fennel is not available, then dandelion is an excellent alternative as it affects the stomach, liver, kidneys and pancreas.

For the Heart

Buckwheat Leaf (Polygonum fagopyrum): becomes wild around areas of cultivation; easily grown or sprouted. Contains rutin; it is very strengthening to the arteries and cardiac muscle. It is an excellent nutritive as well.

Motherwort (Leonurus cardiaca): found occasionally in the wild, common in country gardens. Gentle, calming and supportive to the heart and nerves — it makes an excellent heart tonic.

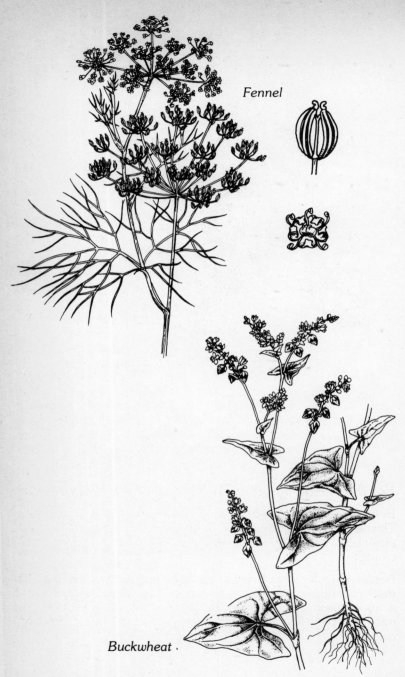

Fennel

Buckwheat ·

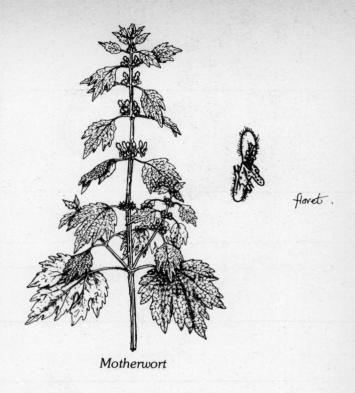

floret.

Motherwort

For the Circulation and Purification of the Bloodstream

Burdock (Arctium lappa): wild and common throughout Britain. This is a major purifier and natural antibiotic. High in easily assimilable minerals and vitamins; coating and soothing to all it contacts.

Nettles (Greater Urtica dioica; Lesser Urtica urens): Perhaps our most common weed and growing abundantly almost everywhere. It is an excellent blood purifier, rich in iron and other vitamins and minerals. It helps assimilate vitamins and minerals, especially calcium.

113

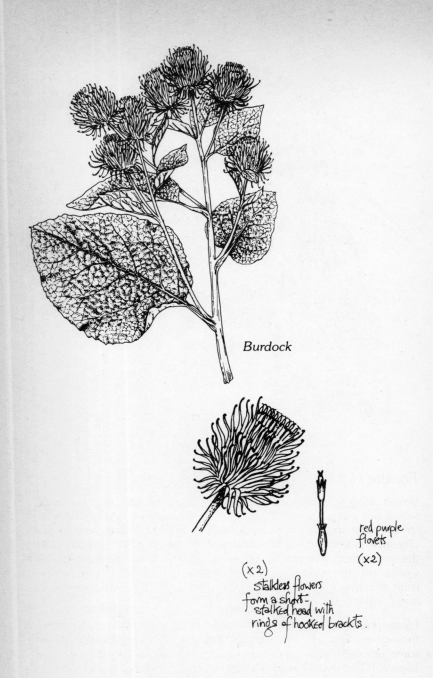

Burdock

(x2)
stalkless flowers
form a short-
stalked head with
rings of hooked brackts.

red purple
flovets
(x2)

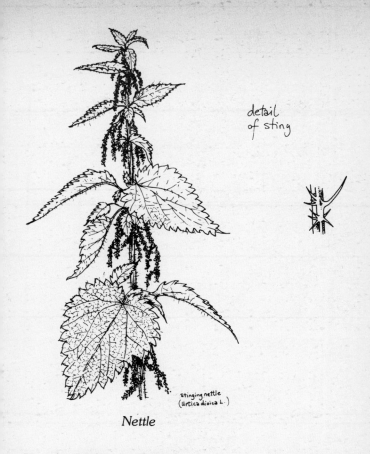

detail of sting

stinging nettle
(Urtica dioica L.)

Nettle

For the Nervous System

Wood Betony (Stachys betonica): reasonably common, wild woodland plant. A safe, reliable nerve sedative, it feeds, regulates, strengthens and rehabilitates the nerve cells, including relaxing the digestive system and alleviating head and face pains. It stimulates the production of nerve fluid, yet calms and heals permanently. It works on the entire nervous system due to its positive yet multidirectional abilities, acting as a nervine, blood purifier, tonic, anti-flatulent, etc, etc.

Hops (Humulus lupulus): wild and common in most hedgerows throughout Britain. A powerful, stimulating, yet very relaxing nerve tonic. It also helps relieve pain and relaxes tense muscles and tissues. It has many beneficial actions in all organs and channels.

115

Wood Betony

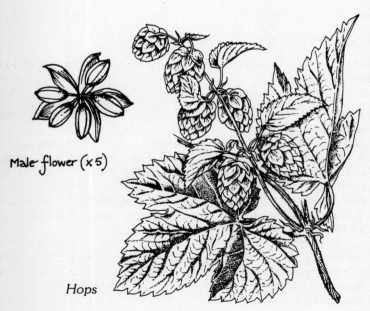

Male flower (x 5)

Hops

THE BLOOD

Second only to keeping the bowel in good order, it is most important that the bloodstream is kept pure and circulating well; if you can achieve these two things then you are well on the way to finding total health. Remember, as the blood carries nutrients so it takes away toxins, and if a bowel cleansing programme is taking place then the bloodstream must be helped to continue the process; so always combine blood purification with a bowel cleanse.

Dr Christopher's Blood Purifying Formula

This formula contains blood rebuilders, cleansers and astringent herbs, while other ingredients remove cholesterol, kill infection or build elasticity in the veins and strengthen the vein and artery walls.
  Mix and powder equal parts of:

Red Clover Blossoms   Oregon Grape Root
Chaparral   Stillingia
Liquorice Root   Prickly Ash Bark
Poke Root   Burdock Root
Peach Bark   Buckthorn Root

Place in a gelatine capsule and take two three times daily.

Blood Purifying Tea

This can either be used to accompany the above formula, or taken more frequently in smaller amounts on its own. It is ideal together with Dr Christopher's Bowel Tonic (page 97).

3 parts Burdock (chopped root)   Major blood purifier, natural antibiotic.
1 part Red Clover (chopped root/leaves)   Generally alterative, it is also a mild stimulant, slightly sedative and able to remove obstructions and act as a detergent; it has potent healing properties.
1 part Dandelion (chopped root)   High in natural minerals and some vitamins, it is also a very cleansing diuretic and makes an excellent blood builder.
1 part Sassafras (chopped root)   Excellent blood purifier. Do not use during pregnancy. After 3 weeks, replace with extra red clover.
1 part Sarsaparilla (chopped root)   Excellent skin and circulation tonic and blood purifier. Contains iron and promotes sweating and the flow of urine.

1 part Nettles (leaves)   High in iron, also contains silicon, potassium, lime, sodium, chlorine and large amounts of protein.

2 parts Yellow Dock (chopped root)   High in iron and a general nutritive and alterative, it draws out toxins and provides a tonic effect.

½ part Liquorice (shredded root)   Excellent blood detoxifier.

1 part Echinacea (shredded root)   The finest antibiotic available.

½ part Yarrow (flowers/leaves in small quantity due to its bitterness) A general diaphoretic (sweat producer), it acts as a tonic and is non-exhaustive (Yin).

Dr Christopher's Blood Circulation Combination Formula

Sometimes extra assistance is needed with the blood purifying teas and formula. There may be allergies present making the job harder, but at any rate, anybody who suffers from cold extremities in the winter will find this a great relief.

Cayenne and ginger feed and stimulate the bloodstream, while the other herbs in the formula assist these two herbs and work together to normalise high or low blood pressure.

Mix together and powder:

3 parts Cayenne
3 parts Ginger
1 part Garlic

1 part Golden Seal
3 parts Parsley

Place in capsules and take two three times daily. After two months replace golden seal with buckwheat leaves and thyme.

Blood Circulation Tea

Poor circulation often means inflexible artery walls which are deficient in vitamins and minerals, and wastes like cholesterol and calcium gather round these weaknesses causing plaque. The narrowing of the arteries causes heart and circulatory strain. Visible signs of this are varicose veins and bruising. Try this tea as a preventive or remedy.

½ part Rosemary Leaves   This herb dilates blood vessels, increasing blood supply to the whole system; it is also nervine and soothes any allergic condition.

½ part Lavender Flowers   Also dilates blood vessels.

½ part Parsley   Very high in Vitamin C, it also contains other vitamins and iron; it is very detoxifying.

2 parts Ginger (flakes)   Stimulant yet carminative to the circulation, it is extremely warming, guiding all the other herbs to the correct area.

1 *part Cayenne* (powder)   This plant amplifies the action of other herbs and as a powerful stimulant it strengthens and regulates the heart rate. It is a cleanser, removes plaque on the walls of blood vessels and stops bleeding. It balances the glands and speeds repair of the heart.

1 *part Sassafras* (replace with ginger or red clover blossom after three weeks. Do not use during pregnancy.)   A highly respected blood purifier, it detoxifies the liver. Its alterative effects greatly help any skin disorders.

Add lemon juice for further blood purification.

Take this tea (1 oz infused in one pint of boiling water for 15 minutes) twice a day with Dr Christopher's formula (see page 118). Or drink it three times a day with capsules made from equal parts of kelp powder and cayenne powder (take two of these at a time). I have already mentioned the beneficial effects of cayenne; kelp (seaweed) helps to rebuild blood vessels; its wide spectrum of vitamins, minerals and trace elements makes it invaluable for all metabolic processes. Its potassium content helps to rebalance salt excesses, reducing adrenal stimulation and hypertension, and potassium is also one of the most essential minerals for proper heart contractions.

Supplements

Other means of helping blood circulation are brewers' yeast tablets (contain B vitamins); spirulina tablets (contain Vitamin B12, but should only be used short-term); cod liver oil capsules (for Vitamin D, needed to absorb calcium, and Vitamin A); wheatgerm oil capsules (Vitamin E, which is the anti-bloodclotting vitamin, helping small veins to dilate and strengthening capillary walls); and lots of fresh parsley in salad and rosehip tea (Vitamin C). Natural Vitamin C tablets are also available from Natural Flow.

Food and Drink

Garlic, ginger and mainly onion soup is also of great benefit to the blood. The oily extract of garlic and onion reduces the tendency of blood platelets to clump together, causing clotting, and aids free movement of the blood generally.

Drink 'Morning Starter' tea (available from Natural Herbal Foods) for blood purification and circulation; for high or low blood pressure use 'China Light' in the same range. For an instant kitchen tea, try paprika, lemon juice and honey. Eating beans of any description lowers blood cholesterol. Eat raw salads at lunchtime: grated beetroot for Vitamin E, grated carrot for Vitamin A; chopped parsley for Vitamin C and chopped onions for sulphur. Use a dressing of onion and apple cider vinegar and lemon juice.

Raw Juices for Blood Purification

Try one glass of this per day for blood purification:

4 parts Apple	1 part Nettle
4 parts Beetroot	2 parts Spinach
2 parts Cucumber	1 part Watercress
4 parts Carrot	

Or, for blood circulation, try one glass per day of a mixture of four parts carrot to one part horseradish.

General Tips

The most obvious aid to all this is plenty of exercise, combined with learning to relax properly. Remember to eat well!

If you feel a great improvement and wish to go on to something easier to take or use for a short-term tonic, then the Gerard House range of pure herb tablets is a good choice. One I would suggest for blood circulation is made from red clover, chaparral and ginseng. Their 'Rutin Plus' tablets are good for varicose veins, high blood pressure and capillary fragility; and as a blood purifier I would also recommend their 'Seaweed and Sarsaparilla Compound' tablets. All are made with natural binders.

Massage also helps to stimulate the blood system, making it easier for the individual to exercise and relax. 'Dry skin brushing' (page 142) and water therapy (page 144) are excellent for blood circulation.

Heart Supportive and Building Tea

Before leaving the subject of blood, I am going to add this formula, helpful in a case of general weakness.

2 parts Buckwheat Leaf Containing rutin, this is very strengthening to the arteries and cardiac muscles. It is an excellent nutritive as well.

2 parts Devil's Claw Rejuvenates and elasticates blood vessels. Normalises high and low blood pressure.

3 parts Hawthorn Berries Helpful to correct low blood pressure, rapid or arhythmic heart beat, inflammation of the muscle; also for insomnia due to heart problems, also varicose veins.

3 parts Ginseng   Excellent heart and circulatory herb, normalises low blood pressure, reduces blood cholesterol.

1½ parts Ginger Root   Stimulant/carminative for the circulation.

1½ parts Comfrey Root   Demulcent; its mucilaginous and cell-proliferant qualities soften and rebuild arteries, muscle, etc.

1 part Cayenne   Food for the circulatory system, it feeds necessary elements into the cell structure of the arteries, veins and capillaries, so that they can regain their elasticity and the blood pressure returns to normal.

2 parts Kelp   Restores elasticity and helps to unlock arteries.

4 parts Motherwort   Excellent heart tonic, calms and supports the heart and nerves.

1 part Coriander   Very strengthening to the heart, adds an interesting flavour.

1 part Vervain   Building in general for a weak heart.

2 parts Centaury   General tonic and heart strengthener.

N.B.: High and low blood pressures: if you suffer from high blood pressure, delete ginseng and liquorice from the above. If you have low blood pressure, delete hawthorn. Add extra cayenne for both conditions. To relieve high blood pressure eat plenty of potassium-rich foods such as potato skins, apple cider vinegar and dandelion and burdock tea.

Now that we have covered the two major reconditioning areas — the bowel and the bloodstream, we will move on to more generalised problems.

Tension and Lack of Sleep

Excessive nervous tension and improper elimination of waste from the body make sleeping and relaxing difficult. Lack of sleep is a major problem as sleeping is itself vitally important to our well-being. Bodily discomforts like digestive and muscular pains, irritability or hormonal excitement, which is pushed by adrenalin inputs, are all symptoms of this complaint.

Nerve chemicals like noradrenalin and serotonin, obtained from foods and herbs, are vital here.

Dr Christopher's Nerve Herbal Food Combination

A wonderful formula for relieving nervous tension and insomnia. It is mildly stimulating and yet reduces irritability and excitement, while also lessening any pain.

Take equal parts of:

Black Cohosh (root)   This reduces pulse rate, calming nerves and muscles. It supplies natural hormones which help balance the glands and prevent them being stimulated unnecessarily.

Capsicum   Prevents irregular flow and blood pressure by encouraging full blood circulation. It also leads other herbs in enhancing and stimulating their activities.

Hop Flowers   A powerful stimulating, releasing nerve tonic. Ideal for pain relief over the entire body.

Lady's Slipper (root)   Revitalises the nerves while tranquillising and sedating. Being a root, it is restorative on a deep level.

Skullcap   A safe, reliable nerve sedative. It feeds, strengthens, regulates and rehabilitates the nerve cells, particularly resheathing the nerve endings. It stimulates the production of nerve fluid, yet calms. Its healing effects are permanent. Slow-working, it should be taken over a long period of time.

Valerian (root)   Sedates the brain and nervous system, but should not be used long-term.

Wood Betony   A nerve tonic and sedative, it also cleanses impurities from the blood, liver and spleen. Vital for removing some of the 'cause' of nervous disorder.

Mistletoe or Elderflower   Mistletoe contains calcium, among other minerals, so important for the nervous system. It is a strong nervine and antispasmodic with gentle anaesthetic properties.
    Elderflower is alterative and stimulant and will quickly remove toxins affecting blood, circulation, lungs, bowels and skin.

Lobelia (root)   A nervine and anti-spasmodic. Internally and externally it relaxes all spasms. Though it is extremely safe, large doses are emetic.

Powder ingredients and place in gelatine capsules. Take two three times a day, with a cup of celery juice or steam distilled water.

This formula contains herbs that feed and revitalise the motor nerve at the base of the skull; herbs that help rebuild and feed the spinal cord; and herbs which rebuild capillaries, nerve sheaths and the nerves themselves.

Sleep and Nerve Tonic Tea

This tea can be drunk quite freely as all the herbs used are quite gentle in their action.
    Take equal parts of:

Skullcap   See above.
Wood Betony   See above.
Elderflower   See above.

Hops   A powerful, stimulating, relaxing nerve tonic. It helps relieve pain and has many beneficial actions in all organs and channels.

Vervain   Excellent for any nervous condition, it also reduces sweating in bed, ridding the body of toxins. Its natural oils sedate and calm the entire nervous system.

Horsetail   High in calcium and silica to refurbish the nervous system.

Lime Tree (flowers)   Soothing, relaxant and slightly sedative but always use freshly dried leaves; old ones produce narcotic intoxication.

Passion Flowers   As a sedative this quietens the nervous system considerably as well as rebuilding it.

Camomile   Calming and soothing to the entire nervous system, sedative in action.

Lemon Balm   For the treatment of nervous disorders in general; soothing and calming.

Nettles   These help assimilate the calcium and provide other vitamins and minerals.

½ an equal part Cayenne   This leads the herbs in, stimulating and enhancing their activities.

½ an equal part Liquorice   The peacemaker.

Note: Include one part burdock if excessive nervous energy is present.

This tea can be drunk at the normal strength either as an evening or night-time drink. Have one to three cups, and drink another tea or fruit juices during the day. Or if the disease is chronic and deep-seated, then this tea can be drunk all day. Five cups a day is a rough guideline for someone of average body weight.

This is a very helpful tea for those who are on sleeping tablets or tranquillisers and wish to wean themselves off them (with their practitioner's help), as the effect of the herbs will match the effects of the drugs. Always reduce your intake of drugs gradually.

Supplements

Calcium is of vital importance in healing the nervous system, building and calming. So take six kelp tablets or calcium tablets (amino-chelated calcium) per day, or as directed by a practitioner.

Cod Liver Oil capsules — for Vitamin D, to ensure calcium absorption.

Zinc is very important and is often associated with a copper excess. For this, use uncooked paprika in your food and eat plenty of whole grains. Using a copper IUD can deplete the body's zinc intake.

B Vitamins are an efficient sleep promoter, so take six brewers' yeast tablets per day — for zinc as well. For B12, use spirulina tablets occasionally, but not for long; other protein intake should be lowered during this time. Alternatively, seek out a Vitamin B complex tablet that is as natural as possible. Gerard House do an entirely natural one, but it lacks folic acid. They also do a folic acid one, as does 'Natural Flow'.

Try cos lettuce or romaine lettuce soup — add a little kelp for flavour; combined they activate the adrenal cortex in its function of secreting the hormone adrenalin to keep the body in balance. The lettuce is a fairly strong sedative.

For a relaxing herbal tea beverage, drink 'Evening Peace', sold in tea-bags by Natural Herbal Foods. Use malted barley (rich in B vitamins) for sweetening.

Gerard House do a Nerve Combination pill of valerian, skullcap, Jamaica dogwood, black cohosh and cayenne; it is useful but because of its valerian content should not be taken long-term.

Raw Juices for the Nervous System

Combine all or some of beetroot, celery, romaine lettuce, spinach, Swiss chard and carrot — one glass per day.

General Tips

Ensure enough Vitamin D intake via sunshine to promote calcium absorption, summer and winter.

Do not eat late at night to ensure that digestion is completed on going to bed. Otherwise, indigestion and flatulence will very likely occur. Obviously you should avoid stimulating drinks and foods — tea, coffee, sugars, salts.

Take a walk half an hour before going to bed, breathing deeply from the abdomen, out rather than in. Start meditation or yoga and try to understand your emotional reasons for sleeplessness. Massage speeds the relaxation process greatly.

If tension and sleeplessness can be overcome, the benefits to other complaints are enormous: nightmares, over-sensitivity, tinnitis, earache, headaches, depression, convulsions, cramp, epilepsy, irritability, migraine, neuralgia, neuritis, asthma, hyperactivity and many many more can be relieved by the above treatments. (See page 145 for more details.)

ARTHRITIS AND RHEUMATISM

Practising as I do in East Anglia, which can be very damp in the winter, I probably see more people with these complaints than I would in other parts of the country, but they are now a national problem.

I often meet people who 'suspect' they might have arthritis or rheumatism and ask what they can do. If you even faintly suspect this and can't get any professional help, for goodness sake, treat yourself as if you had, thus making it less likely or stalling its progress. In any case the treatment will undoubtedly give the body a much needed lift.

External and internal stress are all important to the creation of 'A & R'. They provoke the pituitary gland to stimulate the adrenal stress reaction which raises the levels of sugar, fats and proteins in the blood. This action diverts blood supply from skin and digestion to the muscles — in turn raising blood pressure and provoking the release of calcium (and other minerals) into the blood. Beyond this, uric acid may collect, making the rheumatism worse or producing gout.

The release of the calcium into the blood stream is what causes pain, inflammation and aching, but meanwhile there is also calcium deficiency making irritation, tiredness and insomnia more likely due to the prolonged overuse of anyway dwindling resources of minerals and vitamins in the body.

Dr Christopher's Rheumatism and Arthritis Formula

This formula detoxifies, relieves pain, kills fungus and infection. Most importantly the herbs act as a solvent for the accepted but not assimilated calcium deposits; also supplying herbs rich in newly accepted and assimilable organic calcium.

Take equal parts of:

Yucca	Hydrangea Root
Brigham Herb	Chaparral
Lobelia	Burdock Root
Sarsaparilla	Wild Lettuce
Valerian	Wormwood
Cayenne	Black Cohosh
Black Walnut	

Powder and place in capsules, taking two three times daily.

Arthritis and Rheumatism Herb Tea

As an alternative to the above, try this very tasty tea. Use 1 oz per pint of boiling water, infused for 15-20 minutes. Drink three times a day.

½ *part Cayenne*   Normalises any blood pressure problems.

2 parts Nettles   Ensures intake of calcium into the body, high in iron, potassium and protein.

2 parts Dandelion   Extremely safe diuretic able to flush out toxins. High in natural and easily assimilable minerals.

1 part St John's Wort   Cleansing to the liver, detoxifies, heals and restores tissue, muscle and cells.

1 part Meadowsweet   Acts as a natural aspirin to help with pain. As a very mucilaginous plant it coats and softens inflamed joints. It is also a diuretic, removing acid build-ups.

½ *part Liquorice*   'The peacemaker.'

1 part Burdock   Excellent blood purifier and rich in natural hormones which assist the adrenals.

1 part Comfrey   Important for cell repair and protein content. Helpful for inflammation and rich in Vitamin B12.

1 part Horsetail   Strong diuretic — for removing toxins, acids, etc. High in calcium and silica.

1 part Skullcap   Rebuilds nervous system which is worn due to lack of calcium, helps pain level by calming the whole body.

1 part Sarsaparilla   Excellent blood purifier, contains natural hormones, helpful to adrenals, especially cortin. Contains potassium; is a diuretic.

Herbie's Ointment

We make a lovely ointment using olive oil, beeswax and herbs: cayenne, marshmallow, chickweed, marigold, plantain and comfrey. Olive oil is heated in a double saucepan to above 80°F but not above 100°F. The herbs are then added and left to macerate overnight. Then the mixture is strained and the thick liquid re-heated adding beeswax to harden or firm the mixture.

It is not only useful for A & R. I use it for cuts and burns, dry eczema, shingles, poisons, inflammations, bruises, external ulcers, swellings, etc. Dr Christopher's 'Bone, Flesh and Cartilage' ointment is also excellent for A & R.

Extra Supplements

6 kelp tablets daily   Kelp is vital due to its high calcium content. However, it also promotes glandular health (being good for the thyroid and adrenals). It increases supplies of most vitamins and minerals and especially trace elements, vital for rebuilding enzyme qualities necessary for A & R.

126

2 tsp Apple Cider Vinegar in water (first thing in morning)   Potassium is vital for A & R and this provides a rich natural source.

6 Brewers' Yeast tablets   B vitamins are vital here, especially B5 (or take Natural Flow B5 tablets).

Wheatgerm capsules   For Vitamin E for energy reactions and glandular functions.

 and/or

Evening Primrose capsules   Excellent for A & R; buy from Gerard House.

Devil's Claw tablets   Repair adrenal function and energy levels. Also from Gerard House.

Halibut Liver Oil capsules   Provide Vitamins A and D; particularly useful for rheumatoid arthritis. Also Gerard House.

Additions

Sprouted beans and seeds, celery and celery seed, potato, but particularly potato peeling soup: this has a high mineral and potassium content, vital for A & R.

Sprouted alfalfa seeds contain most vitamins and minerals, eight digestive enzymes and eight essential amino acids, which rebalance glands and blood and build muscle tissue. Rosehip tea, parsley in salads and chewable Vitamin C tablets from Natural Flow provide Vitamin C to help repair adrenal functions and energy levels. Sardines or tuna in oil provide both Vitamin D and calcium, the Vitamin D being essential for calcium to be absorbed.

For a herb tea beverage, drink 'Morning Starter' tea-bags by Natural Herbal Foods.

Raw Juices

Drink lots of carrot juice due to its Vitamin A content, necessary for protein repair, but predominantly celery juice (two pints a day to combat arthritis). Also any of these: cucumber, beetroot, watercress, spinach, nettle.

General Tips

If the body is not too debilitated then an initial one day or three day fast is a good idea (or longer on professional advice). Then go on to a diet with 75% raw food — again as long as the body is not too debilitated. This can change to the ratio detailed in Chapter 3, once marked improvement has taken place.

Try to exercise and meditate. After your condition has improved considerably, if you wanted to go over to herbal tablets and a 'beverage' herbal tea you could. Gerard House do a very good tablet tea called Ligvites, made from herbs and natural binders and helpful in treating rheumatism, fibrositis, lumbago, backache and stiffness of the joints.

Massage is vitally important and acupuncture can be very helpful for rheumatism and arthritis. Make sure the bowels are working properly and work hard on the psyche to discover *why* you have taken on 'A & R'. Read the next section on stress carefully.

STRESS

A normal 'stress response' is an important reaction, yet is only to be used occasionally, when daily life presents us with odd problems or strains, physical and mental. When these occur we want our 'stress responses' to be in full working order and able to cope with the extra needs of the body. Vitamins, minerals and trace elements, used to co-ordinate energy and the activity of all organs and tissues are all the more vital at times of stress.

If the body is drained by constant 'false' stress the adrenals don't function properly, being exhausted and out of balance. Secondary problems like arthritis and rheumatism and other degenerative diseases can arise.

Most of our diet today causes continual stress; a lot of us are on 'red alert' most of the day. For instance white sugar plunges straight into the bloodstream, raising blood sugar levels (hyperglycaemia) very fast — the sugar rush causing hyperactivity, but for what? We are on red alert, bells are ringing, our adrenalin is rushing yet the situation we're in doesn't warrant this. The same happens with tea, coffee, salt and other common western foods. Part of the result of all this is that calcium is stripped from our bones for nerve and muscle use and becomes deposited, unassimilated, in the bloodstream. Apart from a lack of assimilable calcium we also may now be suffering from high blood pressure due to the inorganic calcium dumped into the bloodstream.

Normal stress responses are designed to rebuild the body after the 'adrenalin event', repairing cell damage, returning the blood pressure to normal, replacing vitamins and minerals. Yet over-used, our nutrition levels are not adequate and nervous exhaustion can so easily lead to a complete nervous breakdown.

Remember what I said about stress in Chapter 2, and see also Chapter 6 for alternative therapies.

Dr Christopher's Nerve Formula (see page 121) and the Sleep and Relaxation Tea (p. 122) are very helpful in times of nervous stress, while extra organic calcium is important for nerve sheath repair as well as toning the glands, nerves and muscles, increasing stress resistance and energy while allowing relaxation.

Anti-Stress Tea

For short term use, ideal for very debilitated, fatigued and weak bodies.

1 part Comfrey Root   Aids regeneration of bones, injured by lack of calcium. Generally nutritive and feeding, contains Vitamin B12.

2 parts Horsetail Herb   High in silica which converts to calcium and selenium. It is a strong diuretic so do not overdo dosage.

1 part Lobelia   A nervine and antispasmodic, it relaxes the body and guides the other herbs where needed.

1 part Alfalfa   Rich in all vitamins and minerals and trace elements, including calcium.

1 part Nettles   Vital for the carrying and assimilation of the calcium rich herbs.

1 part Burdock   Will burn up and diffuse excessive nervous energy.

2 parts American Ginseng   Calming, tranquillising, it can have an almost sedative effect.

2 parts Siberian Ginseng (not actually a 'true' Ginseng)   Helps the body to adapt to physical stress, through adaptogens — helping nerves and glands but particularly toning the pituitary gland and adrenal glands. Its effect is 'toned' by the American Ginseng.

2 parts Korean Ginseng   Used as one of the major ginsengs, it promotes glandular balance — especially the adrenals and therefore often helps sexual debility as well! It effects the metabolism in general and helps many ailments and diseases.

Combine the ginsengs, comfrey root and lobelia root and make a decoction (see page 86). Add to an infusion of the alfalfa and nettles. Ginseng root is often treated like a sweet in China, a small piece being chewed in the morning if needed for any reason. If you chew it slowly, say on the way to work, this cuts out the preparation process! Natural Flow do a balanced and useful combination of the three ginsengs mentioned above.
Note: stop taking ginseng once the body's condition has normalised, and never take it for an acute illness as it is Yang in its action.

Extra Supplements

Paprika in gelatine capsules or made into a tea with lemon juice: for zinc, very useful for repair of cell defence response.

Brewer's yeast: Vitamin B5 is vital, but all B vitamins are important. Take six tablets per day. Or use Natural Flow's B specifics.

Kelp tablets: take two three times daily, plus amino-chelated calcium tablets for high dosage calcium to repair the nervous system.

Cod liver oil supplies the Vitamin D needed to assimilate calcium. Rosehip tea, Super C complex or chewable Vitamin C tablets (from Natural Flow) and parsley salad all provide Vitamin C, often drained in the case of nervous diseases.

If great stress and debility are experienced, then high dosage vitamin pills may be necessary; also Raw Glandulars (mixed glandular) as they are fortifying — use the kind produced by Natural Flow.

For beverage herb drink in tea-bags use 'Evening Peace' by Natural Herbal Foods, and eat plenty of sprouted beans and seeds.

Raw Juices

1 glass of combined:

Asparagus	Lettuce
Dandelion	Celery
Nettle	Parsley

or

1 glass of French String Bean Juice.

General Tips

Channel feelings of stress into positive actions through stimulating activities like dynamic meditation, sex or whatever, rather than hating and being angry.

Remember that healthy responses to stress are necessary yet they will not be available if 'over-used' continually.

After a while do relaxing activities like yoga, silent meditation, gardening, walking etc. Try taking Bach Flower 'Rescue Remedy' or give it to someone who you think is under great stress and needs instant help.

Acupuncture changes energies very quickly and this is sometimes very important in bad cases of stress. Otherwise massage is a good idea for relaxing the body yet motivating the metabolism.

DIGESTIVE UPSETS

Indigestion, lack of real appetite, obesity and overeating, flatulence, nausea, ulcers, vomiting; generally bad assimilation of food: the spectrum covered by digestive upsets is quite large and yet we tend to lump them all under this large umbrella.

Appetite is frequently mixed up with our emotions i.e. we eat for comfort, we don't eat if we are worried or whatever. This is because the balance of nerves and hormones communicating throughout the digestive system tells us about our food needs. However, it is frequently ignored, with habits and addictions taking priority.

The stomach itself is a large pouch made up of muscles which produce helpful mucus and acids to aid digestion. Excessive production of either, however, causes impermeable layers for nutrients to pass through and, with the latter, over-acidity. Stress ulcers immediately come to mind here — they are formed when, in times of stress, the adrenal hormones shut down activity, reducing appetite and in turn taking reserve proteins from the stomach walls. We talked of the food processes beyond this point in the early part of this chapter.

Eating too quickly, not chewing your food (so digestive enzymes will not be secreted), bad combinations of food, or insufficient cooking of foods like pulses and beans all bring about indigestion, flatulence etc. So these should be the first points to watch.

Tension held in the jawbone and cheeks (a fairly common problem often demonstrated by grinding of teeth or sucking in of cheeks) will immediately make the stomach become tense as the acupuncture point for the stomach is located around that area. It also makes treating the stomach with acupuncture much harder, due to the tense muscle.

Ulcer Tea

Stomach ulceration is one of the worst of stomach/digestive complaints. Here is a very potent tea to help combat it.

1 part Ginger   Excellent for bleeding and anaemia. Helpful for mucus congestion.

1 part Nettles   Excellent for bleeding and anaemia. Soothing and healing to the mucus membrane, softens and coats stomach lining to protect from abrasions of food fibre.

1 part Comfrey Root   Aids cell proliferation, healing stomach wall linings etc. Helpful to bleeding, soothes generally. Highly nutritious.

1 part Meadowsweet   Acts as a natural aspirin to help with pain. As a very mucilaginous plant it coats and softens. The diuretic action helps remove acids.

1 part Red Raspberry   Mucilaginous qualities coat and protect stomach lining; astringent qualities help any bleeding, while iron and blood building qualities help any anaemia.

½ *part Liquorice* Directs, stimulates and balances other herbs. Promotes healing of gastric ulcers.

½ *part Cayenne* Heals ulcerations, stops any internal bleeding and reconditions tissue. Stimulates digestive juices.

½ *part Oak Bark* Astringent action helps any internal bleeding.

1 *part Plantain* Neutralises stomach acids and normalises all stomach secretions.

1 *part Skullcap* Calms the system reducing stress and excessive production of acids.

1 *part Dandelion Root* Helps counteract stomach acidity by activating liver and bile.

Extras

Also take Aloe Vera juice (made from the gel) as directed, with apple juice to cover the bitter flavour (contains Vitamin B12). Also 'Slippery Elm Tablets' from Gerard House.

Stomach Digestive Tea

This is a more general tea for all other stomach problems:

2 *parts Blessed Thistle* Increases gastric and bile secretion.

1 *part Marigold* Promotes bile secretion.

2 *parts Cinnamon* Stimulates gastric juices.

2 *parts Allspice* Carminative (wind reducing) yet stimulative to digestive juices — a stomachic.

2 *parts Lemon Balm* Calming, smoothing and very good for indigestion generally.

1 *part Ginger* Excellent for any mucus congestion and build-ups.

1 *part Aniseed* Has the same properties as ginger.

4 *parts Dandelion* Stimulates bile, gastric juices, pancreas and is a general liver tonic. Helps counteract stomach acidity by doing so.

2 *parts Papaya* Wonderful for indigestion and over-acidity.

1 *part Skullcap* Calms the system and reduces stress and excessive production of acids.

2 *parts Fenugreek* Comforts and soothes stomach, intestines and nerves, glands and membranes. Contains B vitamins 1, 2 and 3. Important for digestive process.

Supplements

Brewers' Yeast For Vitamin B and zinc — for nerve, muscle and all tissues.

Sprouted Buckwheat For manganese.

Wheatgerm Capsules   For Vitamin E — for muscle tone and healing membranes.

Papaya Plus Tablets (Gerard House)   These are pancreas enzymes and will boost digestion immediately, lowering putrefication, gas and irritation, while improving absorption.

Super C Complex or Chewable Vitamin C (Natural Flow)   Large amounts of Vitamin C help break up cholesterol in the bile, the cause of gall stones.

Fresh Papaya Fruit   use as well as, or instead of, the tea. Useful as a quick initial therapy or when the condition is improved.

Jamaica Spice Tea   A tasty but medicinal herbal tea drink. 1oz to 1 pint Apple juice concentrate (from Suffolk Spice & Herb Company). Use with the Papaya Tablets for a quick remedy of a 'slight' nature. It contains stomachic herbs and spices.

Additions and Food Directions

Cos Lettuce Soup — as much as possible.

Lots of oily fish for Vitamins A and D and calcium. Remember sprouted beans and seeds, whole grains, dark green vegetables etc, especially for zinc.

If you suffer from ulcers, food should contain a certain amount of roughage yet not be abrasive (the same goes for colitis and diseases of the lower intestine). Puree or liquidise if you think food is too rough. The flask whole grain porridge is ideal, also bananas and bananas with live plain yoghurt (the acidophilus in the yoghurt repopulates stomach flora, essential to its proper functioning); and avocados, which are rich in protein and very soft. Initially eat 75% well chopped raw foods or raw juices.

For herb beverage drink 'Lemon Leaf' by Natural Herbal Foods. Take acidophilus tablets from Natural Flow if you want a change from yoghurt.

Raw Juices

Carrot Juice   Vitamin A (for health of mucus membrane lining).

Parsley Juice   Vitamin C (for blood vessels and connective tissue lining).

Cos or Romaine Lettuce   For sedative, calming rejuvenative properties.

General Tips

Remember not to eat, or cook if you are upset, tired or angry. Set out to 'enjoy the meal experience from beginning to end'. Banish any worries from your mind while doing so. Worry doesn't solve problems. Remember that 'tummy problems' are due to fermenting food and putrefaction: visualise the scene and decide it's not for you! Then visualise a perfectly working system, clean and nourished. Thank somebody for the food or meal cooked, show your love and appreciation.

Self-massage of the abdomen is easy, or you can get someone else to do it; try acupuncture and massage all over. Acupuncture can help in severe cases, extremely quickly.

Deep breathing, mostly out from the abdomen is a good idea.

Infection, Colds, Flu, Fever and Upper Respiratory Diseases

This does cover a whole battery of problems, I know; asthma, bronchitis, colds, coughs, hayfever, lung congestion, pneumonia, viral infections, fever, glandular fever, sinusitis, sore throat.

What they have in common is that the upper respiratory system, lungs, nose are being used as the elimination channel instead of the liver, blood and lymph, when waste is excreted primarily through the bowel. One or more elimination channels are blocked (very likely the bowel) and so congestion has arisen elsewhere. Toxic mucus invites bacteria to breed, producing more irritating material. In reaction the system speeds its metabolism to increase elimination, producing a fever (influenza), but also more excess mucus and very often inflammation (laryngitis, bronchitis, meningitis). Irritated mucus membranes are very prone to allergies — dust, pollen, chemicals — resulting in hayfever to name but one.

The cause of excessive upper respiratory mucus is a disorder in the stomach and bowel (see previous sections), so not only does the system need to be cleansed and revived but so do the rest of the eliminative channels.

Another chain reaction from having invited bacteria and virus into our bodies through excess mucus is that our auto-immune system (lymphatic system) starts to react and lymphocytes (protective white blood cells) multiply and release antibodies, to defend and engulf the invading infections. Very often cysts or abscesses are a sign of this. The first cleansing department is the lymph and its white cells, and infection is also often 'contained' in lymph nodes, appendix and tonsils (and some larger vessels). This is a vital safety reaction to stop large scale poisoning — so you see the importance of not having your appendix and tonsils removed!

The thymus gland and spleen add reserves of lymphocytes, for 'really bad occasions', but if you are under stress these reactions do not function properly, and often you will need stress treatment as well.

Lung disorders can come from anguish. Examine the psyche for possible causes, especially with asthma.

First Aid Cold Tea — for the healthy!

If alcohol, exposure to cold or wetness have caused a cold fever, then this very simple tea is excellent. All the herbs promote perspiration, while soothing.

Take equal parts of:

Elderflower
Peppermint
or Yarrow, Catnip, Lemon Balm if these are not available. Make up 1oz to one pint water, drink two cups, get into a hot bath and then straight into bed to induce sweating. Take garlic pearls as well to stop any infection. The cold should be over by the next morning but continue to drink light juices for a while. This tea should only be taken by a healthy person with an acute illness. (For more details, reread pages 72-3.)

Upper Respiratory Tisane

Useful for all disorders.
Note: With a practitioner's guidance, some Lobelia (one to two parts) could be added to this tea.

3 parts Coltsfoot   Very helpful to the lungs in general, bad coughs, asthma and bronchitis.
2 parts Iceland Moss   Excellent for chronic pulmonary problems, tuberculosis, chronic catarrh, its tonic virtues being due to its 'cetarin' content.
2 parts Horehound   Effective for all pulmonary complaints as an expectorant, tonic and diaphoretic helps relieve all congestions in that area.
2 parts Wild Cherry   Remedy for all catarrhal infections, being a general tonic, soothing and yet slightly astringent to the mucus membranes.
2 parts Sage   A cure for infection of the mouth, inflamed sore throat, relaxed throat and tonsils. Helpful for sinus congestions.
1 part Violets   Dissolves mucus, expectorant.
3 parts Mullein   Anti-asthmatic, anti-catarrhal, this plant has a special attraction for respiratory organs and general pulmonary disorders. Being narcotic yet unharmful, it is an excellent pain

killer, calming and soothing, ideal for asthmatics. A most important herb for influencing the glandular system, helping to absorb morbid accumulations.

1 part Echinacea   Acts as the finest antibiotic to remedy infection. (Should be left out of tea, if used long term.)

1 part Vervain   Good for feverish pleurisy, as it induces sweating and relaxes. It is also helpful for colds, flu and coughs, greatly helping to expel mucus.

1 part Marshmallow   Soothing and healing to the mucus membrane, ideal for coughs and pulmonary complaints in general.

1 part Chickweed   Excellent remedy for pulmonary complaints for any inflammation of the mucus membrane — asthma, bronchitis.

1 part Comfrey   Helpful in excessive expectoration of asthma, also coughs, inflamed lung conditions, bronchitis, pneumonia — it soothes and heals all inflamed tissue.

1 part Sarsaparilla   Breaks up mucus and phlegm.

1 part Liquorice   Soothing and softening to the mucus membrane, especially if inflamed, and cleansing of catarrhal infection, especially of respiratory tract. It increases flow of saliva and mucus acting as a decongestant. Helpful for sore throats.

1 part Raspberry Leaves   Very helpful for sore throats by its astringent yet mucilaginous, relaxed qualities.

2 parts Aniseed   Both act as anti-mucus congestant while
1 part Ginger   warming and stimulating.

As you will realise this is a fairly broad spectrum tea, but capable of helping many, if not all, problems in this area. Remember, for a really good dose, infuse one ounce in one pint of water for fifteen to twenty minutes, drinking three cups per day, or make it weaker and have five cups per day. Sweeten with Mexican organic honey.

Dr Christopher's Lung and Respiratory Formula

For generally strengthening and healing these areas and promoting the discharge of mucus, use equal parts of:

Comfrey Root	Marshmallow Root
Mullein	Lobelia
Chickweed	

Powder and place in capsules. Take two three times daily. It is ideal for bronchitis, asthma, tuberculosis, etc.

There is also an excellent Ayurvedic (see page 78) anti-mucus formula. It relieves any congestion immediately and also acts as a natural anti-histamine. It can also be added to other formulas when needed:

1 part freshly ground Black Peppercorns
2 parts freshly ground Aniseed
1 part Ginger Root powder

Add a little honey to form a paste. Take one teaspoonful three times a day before meals.

Lobelia compound tablets, sold by Gerard House, are useful in emergencies. They contain many excellent herbs for the upper respiratory system. Echinacea tablets, also from Gerard House, are useful in case of infection; burdock and garlic are also antibiotic herbs.

Supplements

Halibut or cod liver oil capsules — for Vitamins A and D.
Triple Ginseng Combination (Natural Flow) — use in cases of extreme weakness, debilitation or stress, especially if due to glandular exhaustion. Cease use on recovery.
Brewers' yeast tablets — for B vitamins and zinc.
Kelp — as a general health pick-me-up and for calcium.
Chewable Vitamin C tablets (Natural Flow) — vital for fighting infection.
Papaya tablets (Gerard House) — combine these with echinacea tablets as an antibiotic.
Wheatgerm Oil capsules — for Vitamin E. Overproduction of mucus can cause cysts and this helps to dissolve them. Vitamin E is, of course, important in itself, but it also aids Vitamin C activity.

Additions

Lots of raw food, plenty of sprouted beans and seeds. Onion and garlic soup. Apple juice. For a beverage herb tea drink 'Evening Peace' in tea-bags from Natural Herbal Foods.

Raw Juices

For Vitamins A and C for healing, detoxifying and as an anti-inflammatory, drink carrot, beetroot or parsley juice.

If drug antibiotics have been used to treat the condition, natural bacteria will have been killed, leaving the patient more vulnerable to infection. It is vital therefore that good gastric and intestinal flora is re-established, so eat live natural yoghurt daily for a while, or, better still, acidophilus tablets (two strengths available from Natural Flow)

137

or drink the excess juice from the whole grain porridge as a non-dairy acidophilus (natural yeast) source. Also take apple juice, cucumber juice, onion and garlic juice and papaya juice.

General Tips

The use of antibiotics or fever suppressants will merely bury the problem yet deeper, to be more harmful later on. Remember that the cleansing of other systems and organs of elimination — particularly the bowel — is as vital as dealing with the upper respiratory system.

If you are basically fit, lots of exercise is important during or after this treatment to make sure the lymphatic system can work properly. Massage for those who cannot take exercise is vital, especially a 'lymph drain' — seek out a qualified practitioner for this. Also skin-brush (see page 142). As usual, acupuncture and acupressure are beneficial. Remember that I mentioned earlier that the bowel and lungs were very much connected, physically and emotionally (reread pages 95-101).

Deciding what problems to talk about in this chapter was a difficult thing to do, there being no beginning or ending to the array of illness that herbs can treat. But the above categories cover the most widespread conditions. And the exercise of citing specific problems was not intended to provide immediate home cures and advice but to educate and open the mind. There are many excellent books which cover specifically male or specifically female problems and other less general complaints, and which are a natural progression from this book. See page 157 for some suggestions.

However, I would like to leave you with one recipe which was forty years old when Dr Christopher was given it, so at least eighty years of experience lie behind it now, though probably many more if history had a voice. If this compound were kept in every home and used as the occasion arose, there would be far less sickness.

Dr Nowell's Formula

Ideal for equalising circulation, removing congestions, raising body temperature, easing stomach and bowel cramps; for colds, beginnings of fevers, flu, bowel toxicity, cold extremities, sore throats and much more.

Take equal parts of:

Bayberry Bark   Ginger Root
Cloves   Cayenne Pepper
White Poplar Bark

138

Powder and place in capsules, taking two three times daily.

And finally, an all-round tonic tea, ideal after general recovery has taken place or after specific teas, formulas and treatments have taken effect.

Vitamin, Mineral and Nutritive Herbal Tea

Available loose in Suffolk Spice and Herb Company's 'White Bag' range.

1 part Yellow Dock   High in iron (40%). General nutritive, blood purifier, draws out toxins.

2 parts Dandelion Root   General nutritive, tonic and very high in easily assimilable minerals. Safest diuretic in the botanical kingdom.

½ part Parsley   Contains Vitamins A and B and iron, and is a general nutritive. Also contains three times as much Vitamin C as citrus fruits.

3 parts Alfalfa   Alfalfa is best used fresh; ideally you should sprout it yourself. But dried alfalfa will do as a substitute. It contains most known vitamins and minerals: Vitamins A, B1, B2, B6, B12, C, D, E, K, folic acid, niacin, pantothenic acid, inositol, biotin. Also digestive enzymes and complete proteins. In other words it is nutritionally a most complete plant food.

1 part Rosehip   Very high in Vitamin C.

1 part Nettles   High in iron, also contains silicon, potassium, lime, sodium, chlorine and large amounts of protein. Aids assimilation of other minerals.

1 part Watercress   Add this in freshly chopped. Very rich in most known minerals, especially calcium, also iron and Vitamin D.

1 part Burdock Root   General nutritive and tonic, high in iron and potassium. A natural antibiotic, it also contains natural hormones.

2 parts Comfrey Root   A general nutritive, high in Vitamin B12.

3 parts Elderflower   As a general tonic, it affects the blood, circulation, lungs, bowels and skin, promoting gentle perspiration. A gentle laxative and aperient. It also eases any lung congestion. A good and gentle all-round eliminative herb, quickly removing toxins.

Take kelp tablets with the tea.

This tea is not only rehabilitating and 'good for you', but it tastes delicious; the oil of lemon verbena adds a piquancy to the whole flavour while providing improved digestion and relaxation of the whole body through its soothing aromatic oils.

Cautionary Note on the Use of Herbs

Sassafras   Do not use during pregnancy. Never use for longer than three to four weeks.

Horsetail   Delete from recipe after four weeks, replacing with dandelion. Always combine with a demulcent herb.

Golden Seal   Delete from recipe after two months and replace with thyme or garlic as a substitute antibiotic.

Aloe Juice   This is different from whole aloe vera and aloe gel, which are more potent in their action and can be laxative and produce griping and piles if consumed in the same way as aloe juice.

Garlic Pearls (juice of garlic)   It can be unwise to consume this in cases of high blood pressure, but eating whole garlic does not have such a stimulative effect.

Ginseng/Liquorice   Both stimulate the heart action and should not be taken by anyone with high blood pressure.

Liquorice   Decreases the contraction of the uterus and should not be taken preceding or during labour. Best avoided throughout pregnancy.

Ginseng   Should not be used by those suffering from hot, acute ailments. Use only on a debilitated body and cease when normal health has been restored.

Hawthorn berries   Do not use in cases of low blood pressure.

Essential oils of plants   Use with caution as these are very concentrated forms of the plant. Keep out of reach of children.

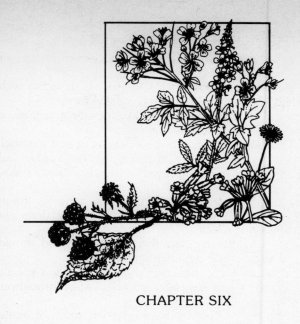

CHAPTER SIX

Further Steps to Self-realisation

BODY MAINTENANCE, CLEANLINESS AND ENJOYMENT

There are many paths to self-realisation, some of which are very close to home and easy to implement. The first category involves nurturing your body on a day-to-day basis. Let's look first at two very basic aspects of daily self-care that are very private and not generally given much thought — washing and sleeping — and one which is more obvious, but which we often think about in the wrong way — dress.

Washing

Proper washing and establishing daily routines can greatly help the healing process. As a major organ, our skin has a two way job, that of protecting the rest of the body from infection and dirt, and that of acting as an elimination channel for toxic waste; working from outside to in and inside to out. This two way job becomes difficult if the skin is sickly, blocked and 'tired' itself. Unhealthy skin is one of

141

the most obvious signs that the rest of the body is not well. Learning to read these signs becomes easy once you've seen what healthy skin should really look like.

Skin Brushing or 'Exfoliation'

Most people's washing is confined to soap and water. Yet this will not remove the layers of dead skin — only gentle and light abrasion on your skin when it is dry will do so. And only if the dead layers are peeled away will the skin be able to live and breathe properly. This activity is called 'dry skin brushing' or 'exfoliation'. It can be a little alarming to the uninitiated, who may feel that they are damaging their skin! But acne, pimples, excessive dryness or oiliness can all be greatly helped by this activity. It also encourages more rapid cell production beneath the surface of the skin. It is a treat and a cossetting experience that I never enjoy missing as it leaves you with that lovely tingling, glowing sensation of a brisk massage! It is in fact the same in body stimulation terms as twenty minutes jogging or twenty minutes Turkish massage and is an ideal way for the lazy, ill or very old to make sure the lymphatic system and bloodstream are exercised.

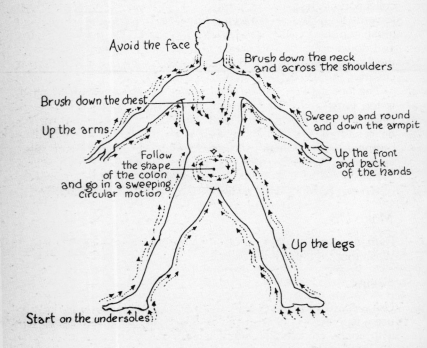

Avoid the face

Brush down the neck and across the shoulders

Brush down the chest

Up the arms

Sweep up and round and down the armpit

Up the front and back of the hands

Follow the shape of the colon and go in a sweeping circular motion

Up the legs

Start on the undersoles

Use a skin brush made from natural vegetable bristles (nylon or animal bristle will be too rough and will damage the skin), with a long but detachable handle so that you can reach your back. Always keep it dry and strictly for this job, washing it in warm soapy water every seven to fourteen days. Brush the body once or even twice a day and preferably in the morning because it is so stimulating. Shower or bath after this.

Skin brushing is a most effective technique for cleansing the lymphatic system (see page 95) through physically stimulating it. It also stimulates the bloodstream and is excellent for poor circulation, and is a vital addition to a colon cleansing programme, helping to dislodge mucus in that area. It takes no longer than five minutes — but don't skimp and do it in less — and can be done while running the bath water. Do not touch the face. Make bold movements, passing only once over each part of the body in a sweeping motion: start by brushing the soles of the feet and work up each leg, up the bottom (avoid the genitals) and up to the middle of the back. That is, work towards the heart and bring all toxins towards the colon. Then start at the fingertips and brush up the arms, across the shoulders, down the chest and the top of the back, again avoiding sensitive parts like the nipples. Do not forget the armpits (a classic point for collection of lymph and glandular inflammation). Again, brush down towards the colon. On reaching the area below the navel, you can brush in movements starting on the right hand side, going up, across and down, following the shape of the colon. Women should brush the breasts (it helps guard against lumps) but avoid the nipples, covering them with the fingertips.

The face should never be skin-brushed in this way, as the treatment is too harsh for it. Wet exfoliation, especially in grimy towns and cities, is a good alternative. This is done during your normal washing, be it bath, shower or hand-basin wash. Use a lotion made from oatmeal and abrasive particles like sand, polyethylene, silica, ventonite or pumice. Once a day is quite enough for the face, preferably at the end of the day to remove grime, grease, etc. I use one made by Mill Creek, available in most healthfood shops.

Make-Up

Remove make-up with an oil or cream cleanser before exfoliating. Wash thoroughly afterwards.

Soaps

Use a soap before exfoliating if you are literally muddy or dirty, but use a type that is pH balanced and won't dry your skin. Experiment with soaps containing natural ingredients such as lanolin, cocoa

143

butter or glycerine; find what suits you best and stick to it. Be guided by ingredients and your skin's reaction to a soap, rather than price. I normally only ever use soap on my hands and feet (the latter in summer with barefoot walking).

The Healing Powers of Water

After washing, whether you have had a bath, shower or hand-basin wash, in warm or hot water, always finish with a cold splash or a 30-second cold shower (avoiding the head unless you are in good health). An excess of cold will deplete energy, yet a quick cold shower revitalises and strengthens it. It does this by causing constriction of the blood vessels, momentarily driving the blood inwards. When you turn off the cold water, the blood rushes to the surface again, warming the skin. It may sound an unpleasant experience but it is really rather nice. How often do you feel exhausted and tired out after a hot bath? This way you'll feel relaxed yet revitalised while resistance to general illness will be much increased. Catching a cold or chill will be quite out of the question.

Putting Epsom Salts and herbs into the bath is further stimulating, reviving and rejuvenating, as well as adding a luxurious feeling to the experience. I regard a hot bath and quick cold splash as the best 'relaxer' on offer.

You should have a complete body wash *twice* a day, being one of the best 'preventive' ill health routines.

Deodorants

These are often put on after washing in the belief that they will be needed sometime later to cover up bodily smells and stop the sweating process. Not only are they harmful to the body in that they block a major elimination channel, but they are also unnecessary in a clean, detoxified body. Smells are a sign of ill health and we should tackle the cause rather than covering up the symptoms. The same applies to vaginal deodorants, often used during menstruation; excessive menstrual odour means extra attention must be paid to cleanliness or indeed a blood cleanse (see blood purifying teas, Chapter 5) should be undertaken. If you work in a hot, poorly ventilated office or take part in a lot of sports, then the job of washing needs more time and vigilance. You can always wash in a toilet for privacy; carry a damp flannel in a bag around with you.

Tampons and Sanitary Towels

Tampons are generally known to build up smells, as stale blood stays in the vagina (its natural passage being down and out). Tampons can cause tremendous irritation and heat build-ups,

144

making problems like cystitis and thrush far more likely. Use instead one of the modern sanitary towels that stick unseen to the knickers, and change frequently.

Hair

Keeping your hair clean is as vital a task as keeping your skin clean. We are often told that washing it too often will strip vital oils from it, and if the wrong shampoos are used then yes, this is so. But using natural shampoos daily merely keeps the hair clean and glowing. Go for organic, soap-based, herb or cider vinegar combination ones. Incidentally, using commercial conditioners is one of the worst things you can do to your hair. They are often based on plastics which do indeed coat the hair, giving it body and sheen, yet deteriorate it at root level, blocking pores in the head.

Feeding the Hair

Giving it colour, texture, body and sheen the natural way is easy. Take natural B vitamins in the form of brewers' yeast tablets, or B complex from Gerard House or Natural Flow; malt barley, blackstrap molasses and whole grains. (Synthetic B vitamins cannot be absorbed and assimilated, although there are B vitamin pills made from natural substances.) Also use seaweed in your diet, either in soups or in the form of kelp tablets. Sulphur will also give your hair sheen and foods like watercress, cauliflower and onion are rich in sulphur.

Sleep

Enough sleep is vital to our rejuvenation, as it is while we are asleep that cells build and repair, and organs and systems rest. Our dreams can perform the nightly task of sorting out the day's unsettled problems, emotions and thoughts. 'Early to bed, early to rise' is an old but very wise saying. Going to bed at ten o'clock is the ideal time. Sleeping between the hours of ten and midnight gives us the equivalent of four hours sleep, compared with midnight to two o'clock which is much less rejuvenative. Therefore you could theoretically rise at five o'clock in the morning feeling adequately rested. Getting up at six o'clock is a little more civilised and an excellent time for meditation, followed by exercise, chores or hobbies before the pressures of the day begin. One suddenly finds one has the 'time' and the 'energy', often two excuses for not doing anything. If you have young children or babies you will naturally find yourself wakened by them at these times. Train them to occupy themselves in their cot or playpen while you give *yourself* some time. Or ask your partner to look after them — sharing of 'time off' is important when young children are around.

145

I was told by one of my teachers always to sleep on my left side (encourage young babies and children to do this). The left side of the body is Yin — cool and less active — while the right side is Yang, very heating and will produce energy and restlessness.

Difficulty with Sleeping (see Chapter 5 for herbs to help)

There is a connection between sleep and water which is helpful for poor sleepers. Fill your bath three to four inches full of cold water! Make sure the bathroom is warm, however. Put on a woollen cardigan or jumper to cover the top half of your body. The aim is to get your *hips* and *bottom* into the water, so you can either sit in the bath normally or dangle your legs over the side. This can even be done in a deep bidet. Sit there for thirty seconds only, then quickly dry yourself, putting on cotton nightclothes or sleeping nude if it is warm enough, in cotton sheets and natural fibred bedding. This sort of bath is called a *Sitz* and what it does is to draw the blood away from the head, bringing release from tension and giving calm and relaxation. 'Urtication' with stinging nettles was once used for this.

Being too hot or too cold can produce restlessness in bed; excessive sweating is often the result of synthetic fibred bedding. The optimum bed temperature for sleep is 84°F and natural fibres help to maintain this. The mattress should be of natural fibres, as well as sheets and blankets. If your mattress is synthetic (foam or sponge etc), you can use 100% pure cotton quilted sleepers which tie on the mattress between you and it.

Sleep and Barefoot Walking

Perhaps an unlikely activity at the dead of night but an excellent answer for insomnia. It expends static electricity through the soles of the feet, while heat is also drawn downwards from the head. Do it for about three to five minutes on grass, sand or soil; then dry your feet and put on dry shoes and socks or slippers for a few minutes, then pop back into bed.

Barefoot walking, even walking in the snow, should be an everyday remedy for sleeping problems. Winter or summer, try it and see how good it is! Chilblains will be a thing of the past. However, never allow yourself to get damp or chilled, otherwise you will go beyond the stimulating effects to potentially harmful ones.

Even for those with no sleeping problems, barefoot walking should be a part of each day.

Shoes

This leads me on naturally to the subject of clothes. We all too often consider fashion to the detriment of health and shoes are a prime example of the damage we can do to ourselves. When we aren't walking barefoot on grass, sand or soil, then correct shoes are vital. As our feet function best when walking on these natural mediums then a shoe should mimic these as far as possible. Our feet were not designed for high heels, for instance — they cause calf muscle contraction and eventually permanently shorten these muscles, causing stiffness and inflexibility. This in turn causes imbalance throughout the whole body, affecting the spine, head position etc, and influencing the way we think and feel. Contoured, breathing, supportive shoes, suitably warm or cool, are a fine investment, while anything that causes sweating, chaffing and aching feet, should never be considered. If you must wear 'smart' damaging shoes then confine their wearing to the odd occasion, returning as quickly as possible to your comfortable footwear.

Natural Fibres

I mentioned wearing cotton in bed and the same applies at other times of the day. The wearing and general usage of natural fibres allows free air circulation, enabling the body to breathe. Finding all silk or all cotton underwear can be quite a problem but once you have tracked down a source, stick to it. Wearing silk stockings is a much more tactile experience anyway, than suffocating nylon ones! Pure cotton and wool clothes are much more easy to come across, especially with Indian cotton imports and the fashion for woollen jumpers made here and abroad. If it is important for adults to wear natural fibred clothing, it is vital for children and even more vital for babies. General well-being is hard enough for adults to understand, but the young cannot formulate these ideas and often take overheating, skin irritation and other problems encouraged by synthetics for granted. While sadly many cot deaths can be explained by synthetic fibres suffocating the baby's skin, which is a vital life support system much needed when other organs are still forming.

All this advice, do's and don'ts may seem overwhelming at first but once, little by little, the routines are established then your feeling of general well-being will show you why changes are vital.

Let us now consider an aspect of self-realisation and well-being which goes deeper and which will require more effort on your part.

OTHER METHODS OF SELF-REALISATION

Self-realisation is a very important part of personal development and it is not until we know ourselves, our demons, faults and good points that we can actually forget the word 'I' and start helping other people. This should not be done in a self-conscious way like the village 'do-gooder' or 'Lady Bountiful', but as a genuine and natural progression in yourself where phrases like 'my depression' or 'my headaches' start unconsciously disappearing from your vocabulary. Don't be afraid of the very necessary self-indulgence of putting yourself under examination. Treat it as a vital part of self-development so you can be more useful to, loving towards and loved by others. Remember to give yourself a little time for rejuvenation each day or week as part of a balanced approach to daily life. Your batteries will be used by others as well as yourself, and they must be recharged and even reviewed at times. 'Self-realisation' can take many forms, from having your astrological chart done to climbing the highest mountain in the world. Let's start with an outlet that is available to almost everybody:

Exercise

Exercise as a form of self-realisation can produce many results in many different ways; each therefore to their own. Physical well-being produces mental well-being and this has been understood by many nations for many centuries. However, it is also frequently forgotten as being a vital part of our daily lives.

If you already have a physically demanding job then choose an exercise which releases the mind or greatly relaxes the body, using muscles not used during your job, so a balance can be maintained and your mind relaxed. Most exercise tones most systems and organs, while all have a beneficial effect on the respiratory system, through exercising the respiratory muscles, diaphragm muscles, the intercostal rib cage muscles and stomach muscles; *all this aids the movement of oxygen, our most vital life-force.*

Exercise also aids the nervous and endocrine systems, the brain and spinal cord, muscles, skin, joints, heart rate, gastric functions and glandular secretions. The circulatory system will work harder preventing hardening of the arteries and weakened heart muscles; and so on and so on.

Simple activities like walking and cycling (preferably amongst trees and grass, not streets and buildings) are two excellent ways of rejuvenating oneself physically and mentally. The list of good points is unending, but perhaps number one is fresh air, with the exchange of oxygen washing the brain and flushing the bloodstream. The actual activity of the muscles works on the lymphatic system, which, unlike the bloodstream, driven by the heart, needs physical effort to ensure that it carries out its job of defending the body with its auto-immune sensitivity.

Gardening is a wonderfully creative art and should form part of the life of a 'living herbalist', literally growing your own health. Few activities exercise the muscles in the middle of the lower back the way that gardening does. However, always take things gradually: sudden violent exercise will give you backache, but if you start off gently with a gradual build up of activity, the exercise is highly beneficial. Gardening means the constant use of hands and arms, exercising the muscles and increasing mobility in the elbows, wrists and finger joints. Moreover, the joy of watching things grow is a nourishing experience, and if you are growing vegetables or fruit as well as flowers, eating your own organic produce is a further benefit. If you haven't a garden of your own then lend yourself to someone who has, or try and obtain an allotment.

Jogging is popular nowadays but it should be taken in a relaxed manner and done preferably on grass, while you should be an experienced 'walker' before taking it up. Initially walk and jog, walk and jog, to warm up. Your pace should allow you to talk while jogging and if you are not able to do this, because you are out of breath, then you are pushing yourself too hard and should slow your pace until your body catches up with your mind! Jogging should be done in a 'springing' motion — pretend you are jogging on a trampoline (bouncing on a home trampoline in front of an open window can be an alternative to jogging and is often much better for your spine) while the back should be kept erect (imagine each vertebra pulled out to its full extent) and relaxed, avoiding a hunched, 'leaning forward' posture. The shoulders must be relaxed. So often joggers have a grim, determined expression on their faces, with their bodies lurching forward violently towards their goal. This is not the correct approach. Jogging in the morning before breakfast is ideal, avoiding food indigestion and giving you a lovely fresh and energising start to the day. Concentrate on breathing out rather than in. Swimming, dancing, any such activity will greatly benefit the system, and can be taken up by almost anyone at any age. If you are retired you may find that you have lots of time on your hands — so leisure and relaxation can really be worked at! Swimming is the most universally exercising to the whole body, providing the best aerobic exercise.

Whichever form of exercise you take up do it gently, find out about it and talk to people who really understand about the effects of exercise on the body. If you have been ill, ask professional advice before taking exercise, in case your body is not strong enough to cope. Listen to your body constantly, and learn from its reactions.

There are forms of exercise that seem to come under a different heading in people's minds than those already mentioned and which work more directly on the psyche. Let me start with one that is not so much exercise but a fundamental to exercise, involving the correct way to move, stand and walk.

The Alexander Technique

'Every man, woman and child holds the possibility' for physical perfection, it rests with each one of us to attain it by personal understanding and effort.' F.M. Alexander 1869—1955

This technique is concerned with the way in which we use ourselves. The idea is that during our daily activities, we are making use of highly involved instruments — our bodies. Most of the time we do not consider that we have anything to learn about the way our bodies work or the way we use ourselves. Alexander found that the way we feel is the result of habits in the way we use our bodies and because they are habits, they have constant influence on us for good or ill. All our 'doing' actions are reliant on our feelings, and often that 'feeling' monitor is wrong, with awkward habits learnt since late babyhood. The technique is concerned with learning, or re-learning an improved relationship with the way we control ourselves. Young babies naturally move correctly but they soon learn to copy their parents' faults, ensuring another generation of bad movers! The dynamic relationship between the head and the neck and the relationship of these to the back is a primary control. Simple tasks like picking things up off the floor correctly, getting out of a car — all these are the Alexander Technique's province. The human body, with its mechanisms for balancing upright on two legs, is capable of moving with remarkable lightenss and freedom. This is scarcely surprising when we remember that it is the product of millions of years of evolution. But if we do not master this art of balancing we must habitually make up in muscular effort what we lack in natural poise.

Alexander's discovery, that a certain quality of freedom and balance in the relationship between the head, neck and back is responsible for this poise, offers us the means to improve our own manner of using ourselves. The quality referred to, which is not a fixed position, is as much mental as physical. Interference with this freedom and balance brings about a deterioration in movement, sensitivity and health. Conversely, any return to it improves our physical, mental and emotional condition.

The individual is the focus of the Alexander Technique. We are all unique, with different bodies, different experiences and different problems. We go about the process of change in different ways and at different rates. For these reasons the practice of the technique is taught on a one to one basis.

What happens in an Alexander lesson depends very much on the needs of the student at the time. But basically we have to unlearn the attitude of trying to achieve our ends quickly at any cost. Instead we have to care about taking time to think of how we can best set about doing what we want to do.

In a lesson the student learns to experience this in a practical way through the teacher's hands. The use of the hands is not like massage or any forceful manipulation, but rather a gentle guiding of the body into a new, more balanced, poised state. Through this experience the student gains the opportunity to choose whether to continue in this new way or to revert to the old habitual way that feels so familiar.

Obviously, since what we are changing are patterns built up over many years, a permanent change will not be brought about overnight. However, the person who learns to stop and take time, to think constructively about how he uses himself in everyday life, will find that this simple procedure can have far reaching results.

The Alexander Technique is not a royal road or a panacea. It is not even mainly a therapeutic technique for it is not designed to bring about remedies or cures except by indirect means — that is, by becoming aware of, and learning to prevent, the harmful habits that cause us unnecessary stress and restrict our capabilities. And, then, by learning to replace these harmful patterns with consciously and creatively chosen ones.

The Alexander Technique is taught at many colleges of music and drama and used in a great variety of ways to improve performance in such diverse skills as athletics, riding, golf, singing and dance, yoga, and many other aspects of professional performance and personal growth.

Information about teachers of the Alexander Technique may be obtained from
The Society of Teachers of the Alexander Technique (S.T.A.T.), Suite 10, London House, 266 Fulham Road, London SW10 9EL.

Yoga

Yoga is an ancient practice going back to at least 600 BC and nowadays provides a perfect way to give yourself a relaxed mind and body, supple and controlled and encouraging peak physical fitness. Although peak physical fitness is a good thing, yoga should more often than not be called 'yoga exercises' as this is to a large extent all that is left of this ancient art form. All the correct breathing patterns are rarely taught and these should come before any exercise. The spiritual side of yoga is also almost entirely neglected — yoga exercises are only the positions that previous yogis found spiritual illumination in!

However, the postures do tune up the body in general, exercise and massage internal organs and glands, enhance the circulation and calm the nervous system. There are 120 true postures that can be used to achieve these ends, although over 400 have been concocted recently! Yoga can aid efficient daily breathing and also teach some special kinds of breathing helpful for deep relaxation. (So even 'superficial' yoga is better than nothing.) Yogis say, 'He who only half breathes, half lives.' The result of all this is increased stamina, improved co-ordination and balance and better posture. The attainment of balance aids the powers of concentration, with mind and body helping each other continually.

Yoga can be started at any age from four to 94, but the body should never be strained: it should be stretched to its capacity, but not pushed beyond that point. Daily practice makes for safe and gradual progression and all that is needed is a small or large airy room. Leave at least two hours gap after the last meal before starting any yoga.

Always talk to someone who is qualified in yoga practice before commencing it. Some positions are harmful to, say, high blood pressure, while others can particularly help problems like excess weight by activating the thyroid and metabolism.

What I personally like about yoga is its gentle, yet stimulating approach. Amongst the many kinds to choose from, 'Chinese Yoga' seems to me to be the best. The breathing techniques it uses allow greater massage and lubrication of the internal organs amongst other things. But search around and find out which most suits yourself. Yoga teaches a commitment to doing everything as well as one can, whether it is the washing-up or flying an aeroplane; giving a pride and purpose to life, enriching it for yourself and those around you.

Tai Chi Chuan

Tai Chi Chuan or 'Tai Chi' is a martial art form made up of exercises based on the forces of Yin (female, negative) and Yang (male, positive) as expressed in fight.

Tai Chi, or Yin-Yang theory is the unifying principle that runs through the whole Chinese culture. The 'Chi' part of Tai Chi means energy, the kind of energy that sometimes manifests itself in the form of various sensations. For a beginner in Tai Chi heat, sometimes quite intense, is the most common feeling. It is a wonderful activity for those with an aggressive nature who learn to balance this by understanding their imbalances through the movements; or those with a repressed, fearful nature, unable to express their emotion; they too will achieve balance. Mental attitudes are explored through exercise, as are balance and the senses; with faulty balance being corrected. Patience is required, as the impatient will soon learn, while practice is fundamental.

An advanced form of Tai Chi involves exercise to increase one's sensitivity to direction, force and speed of movement, and was originally meant as a preliminary to sparring in self-defence training.

Like all good forms of exercise, the postures and movements of Tai Chi should be adjusted to suit individual capabilities and requirements. The physical effort required to do the exercises is greater, the lower the stances and the slower the exercises. For this reason, a relaxed body with no tension is important.

So what is Tai Chi? It is mainly involved with a physical and mental attitude; a kind of kinetic meditation. Its practice, like some of the other exercise arts mentioned, aims to lead us to a realisation and appreciation of the spiritual side of our natures. The experience is similar to that of an enlightenment and religious experience but Tai Chi as a discipline does not have any spiritual or religious dogma; like all these teachings it allows the individual to find his or her own path.

It is important in learning anything to distinguish the means from the ends. One common mistake among beginners is to try hard to achieve the 'ends'; to gain 'spiritual materialism' as I call it! Or just to please the teacher, as we are taught when we are young. Remember, in this case, it is the journey that is the most important thing, giving yourself up and just letting it happen.

Autogenic Training

Based on control over the autonomic nervous system, it is in essence a form of meditation, but one that has become very popular. It is particularly useful for people who simply won't or can't go in for any of the aforementioned exercises, techniques etc, because it can be done anywhere at any time — in a train, in the office, during a tea break or whatever — lounging in an easy chair in a slumped 'rag-doll' attitude or lying on your back with your arms at your sides. Its benefits are colossal, as it calms the nervous system and brings down stress levels or relieves acute fatigue. It is very useful for arresting asthmatic attacks and other such seizures, instead of resorting to an inhaler. Its aim, unlike some meditation exercises, is specifically to induce simple physical sensations. These are intended to lead to a state of relaxation of a purely physical nature: slowing the heart beat, reducing blood pressure and improving the depth of respiration. In all, old tensions are eliminated or discharged and occasionally the muscles in the arms and legs (as they relax) twitch for a few moments. As with all other meditative exercises, autogenic training is best taught by a trained teacher.

Assume your preferred posture (those in wheel chairs can do the slumped doll posture) and with as little outside disturbance as possible, close your eyes and focus attention on your arms. Taking one arm at a time, suggest to yourself that it is heavy, several times. Cover the entire body like this. In all there are six steps to go through in this manner, the first two being to suggest relaxation of each limb and then to feel warmth in each limb. The 'session' takes about ten to fifteen minutes and the result, once the technique has been successfully mastered, is a feeling of profound, deep relaxation. You can use this for the rest of your life. You must however be guided by a teacher to master this to avoid bad habits; reading about it is not good enough.

Meditation

There are so many forms of meditation one cannot possibly go into them all. We have briefly discussed some popular 'named' varieties of meditation but a deeper understanding of the entire reason for meditation is often lacking, while many people 'bent on meditating' often find they cannot. The best way to learn how to meditate is to learn how not to. Again, find a good teacher who can explain this. Meditation should happen as a birthright, yet from birth, it is interfered with. Therefore, we have to be 'taught' methods and approaches to lose our consciousness. This merely means learning not to think or use our intellect, learning instead to let go until our instinctive intelligence takes over. The intelligence taking over from the intellect is known as meditation. This is, of course, the hardest part of all and much time has to be spent discovering what may be blocking your ability to do this.

Meditation is a wonderful art, creating harmony and balance within ourselves and producing better, more enjoyable surroundings for everyone else. The 'tipping of the scales' in violent down or up swings instead of the gentle sway of the pans rising from a solid base, is as wrong as violent, eruptive anger or suppressed, inverted resentment. Yet so often we are slaves to these feelings. Natural

154

fluctuations of emotions are healthy and healing and experiencing many different feelings and sensations is all part of life. It is, therefore, important in meditation to explore the emotions we hate in ourselves. In other words, it's no good practising silent meditation when deep down inside we are longing to scream. Noise comes before silence and the first step, therefore, is to find a form of meditation that brings all this out — 'dynamic meditation'. This often means the 'storm' before the 'calm'. But, as with the other changes of diet and lifestyle discussed in this book, the effort required is amply rewarded by the results.

I was lucky enough to find an excellent teacher of meditation who shows all his students the many methods of achieving that 'loss of consciousness'. It can be through dancing, chanting, silence or whatever personal 'trick' will lead to that state, if only for twelve seconds. He also taught us that past experiences of illumination can never be repeated nor should they be sought (every experience being new and different). So whatever happened yesterday may not be the case today. No true experience can be gained in under forty minutes and that is why giving yourself an hour of personal time every day for your various efforts is vital. However, practice can start with just five minutes a day in order to establish a routine or pattern, and you can increase this as your will or needs dictate. The earlier section on sleep will show you how extra time in the day can be achieved without loss of sleep or tiredness.

Now to finish with:

FOUR GOLDEN RULES FOR LIFESTYLE AWARENESS

. . . all of which I have had to work towards just as much as you!

Yes and No

These two words are the two many of us find most difficult to use at the appropriate time. We say one while meaning another from early childhood in order to please or because we are angry. Learn to say *no* in an assertive, non-aggressive way. Doing this will banish all those misconceptions about being 'nice' and 'going along with everyone else'. All repressive feeling and self-deception will disappear, giving way to true emotions and the joy of saying a real *yes* when we mean it. Likewise learn to say an honest *yes* without weighing up the odds overmuch, or working out the gain or loss factor. A genuine *yes* means people accept *no* as genuine too, and they respect this and feel much more comfortable. Friendships and family flourish on it.

Openness

In order to assimilate any of the ideas talked about in this book you have to open up the mind and create a space for new ideas. If your mind is full of preconceptions and chatter there can be no room for new ones. That is not to say that one should become a sponge, allowing everything to enter the mind indiscriminately. Your openness of mind should be unconditional in the sense that you should listen in an open way to any suggestions you may hear, rejecting them afterwards if your emotions or the information available seem to advise this. Many of us have the terrible tendency to be sheep-like in our reaction to life in general, but never entirely surrender to any experience, while others talk inanely, regurgitating old ideas, afraid to allow room for new ones.

Laughing

Learn to laugh first at yourself and then at life in general (but not unkindly at other people's expense). Laughing at yourself frees you of the self-importance which goes with a 'serious' view of life. Spontaneous joy and laughter is perhaps the greatest gift of man, while lack of or suppression of 'belly laughter' can cause much illness.

Love and Compassion

Caring for others is the only way to prevent conflict on an individual or a worldwide scale. Learning to let go of fear and replacing it with love, firstly learning to love yourself, will help you to follow the suggestions in this book quite naturally. Open up your hearts.

Useful Books and Addresses

There are now an enormous number of books on herbs and on alternative medicine, but I have selected a few which I like and which are appropriate to each chapter, along with addresses of organisations or suppliers you may find helpful or interesting.

Chapter One

Books

Green Pharmacy by Barbara Griggs
An incredibly informative book on the history (pre-historic to present day) of herbal medicine, its ups, downs, prejudices and praises — enjoyable reading too.

Transformer Magazine
Concerned with new lifestyles, changing times, natural ways to live and grow. Compiled by members of the New Health Movement. Write to: New Life Designs Ltd, 159 George Street, London W1H 5LB.

New Health Magazine
A new publication — very modern and current, capturing some people who might otherwise have walked on.

Here's Health Magazine
Available on every bookstall, a very informative magazine of long standing.

Grace Magazine
A truly holistic magazine, gentle, sophisticated and slightly old-fashioned, yet endearing and relaxing for that quality. Available in many healthfood stores.

Natural Medicine by Brian Inglis (Fontana)
He discusses the progress of all natural medicine from pre-Christian times to the present day, bringing us up to a comprehensive guide to the many natural therapies now available.

Back to Eden by Jethro Kloss
A simple (now old) homely book about a man, his family and their views on nature — cures and natural healing. He did a lot to start our present day interest in the subject. Available from Thorsons Publications Ltd, Dennington Estate, Wellingborough, Northants.

Medicine for Beginners by Tony Pichock and Richard Clark
Available from Newman Turner Books

Chapter Two

Books

I Want to Change but Don't Know How by Tom Rusk and Randy Read
A comprehensive handbook for mastering change — offering practical and accessible methods. Available from: 'Changes Bookshop', 14 St Michaels Hill, Bristol BS2 8DT. Tel: (0271) 211792.

How to Change Yourself and Your World by R. Evison and R. Horobin
A manual of co-counselling and theory of practice. A good starting point for self development. Available from Changes Bookshop.

Inner Journeys
Visualisation in growth and therapy. A very touching, helpful book about inner journeying. Available from Thorsons.

Love, Hate, Fear, Anger by June Callwood
Our emotions explained, suppressions realised. This book is a helpful insight. Available from Thorsons.

Addresses

The Association for Humanistic Psychology in Britain
62 Southwark Bridge Road
London SE1 0AS
It holds workshops, discussion groups, etc and is interested in alternative lifestyle, human potential, ecological responsibility and so on. It has a two-monthly magazine called *Self and Society*.

Rajneesh Association of Holistic Medicine
Medina Rajneesh
Herringswell
Bury St Edmunds
Suffolk IP28 6SW
Tel: 0638 750254
and Medina Rajneesh Body Centre
    81 Belsize Park Gardens
    London NW3
    Tel: 01 722 6404/8220
Spiritual growth, self-awareness, all kinds of natural healing therapies.

The Metamorphic Association
67 Ritherdon Road
Tooting
London SW17 8QE
Tel: 01 672 5951
The Metamorphic treatment is a simple approach to self-healing and creative growth. The centre holds workshops, lectures etc.

The Centre for Attitudinal Healing
31 Craven Street
Trafalgar Square
London WC2N 5NP
Tel: 01 839 7481
Group meetings share common fears and anxieties and explore positive approaches, games, creative visualisation etc. A good book available from the centre is *Love is Letting Go of Fear* by Dr G. Jampolsky.

HUG Harmony, Unity, Goodwill
A Fordeah Project. For further information on 'The Game of Hug' contact:
Lizanne Davies
Fordeah
1 Hinde Street
London W1
Tel: 01 486 8244
Workshops, lectures or 'help'.

Rebirth Society
The Secretary
The Rebirth Society
21 Streets Heath
West End
Woking
Surrey
Tel: Chobham 7243
Rebirthing is a healing method, which gives you the experience of mastery in your life — noticing that your experience of life derives from your thoughts about life and that you can change these thoughts is a basic step.
  The society has a list of some fifty qualified rebirthers all over the country.

Play-World: A Centre for Mind and Body, Health, Growth and Fitness
58 Westbere Road
London NW2 3RU
Tel: 01 435 8174
'Laughter is catching, joy is infectious'; find out more at the above address.

Relaxation for Living
Hon. Secretary
Dunesk
29 Burwood Park Road
Walton-on-Thames
Surrey RT12 5LH
Tel: Walton 227826
A centre for physical and mental relaxation.

Healing Through the Soul
Dr Louise Sand and Inga Hooper
18 Cedar Road
Sutton
Surrey

Tel: Leatherhead 379168 (day)
   01 643 4255 (evening)
A centre for healing through the mind using the heart, the soul; the person is made aware of his or her true nature. A higher level of consciousness is reached from where the person can take off like a rocket!

Network
Provides a way to start changes and meet like-minded people. The aim of these various groups is to link together groups and individuals who are seeking a deeper understanding of life and the art of living, and the holistic development of man and his harmonious and unifying relationship with his fellows and the planet. Groups are in the Cotswolds, London, the South-East, the South, East Anglia, the North and Wales.
Contact Catriona Striberry
or Christopher Russell-Powier
91a Clarendon Road
London W11 4JG
for information about your area. Network also have a networking journal called *Link-Up*. Sir George Trevelyan gives much of his time and effort as many others do to this whole enterprise.

Bach Flower Remedies Ltd
Dr E. Bach Centre
Mount Vernon
Sotwell
Wallingford
Oxon OX10 0P2
There are 38 remedies covering every negative state of mind known to man; all can help change attitude and provide self discovery. The book *Heal Thyself* by Dr Bach discusses some of the emotional causes and cures of disease.

Music for the Pure Joy of Listening
Gentle relaxing music, to ease you into a state of inner peace and harmony. For a free catalogue write to:
Good Vibrations
122 Latchmere Road
London SW11 2JT
Tel: 01 228 9820

The Human Integration Centre
5 Phillmore Terrace
Allen Street
Kensington
London W8 6BJ
Tel: 01 937 6632
Help on all emotional fronts.

160

National Federation of Spiritual Healers
Old Manor Farm Studio
Church Street
Sunbury-on-Thames
Middlesex TW16 6RG
They have a Healing Review to all members.

Healing and Astrology
Deep
Garden Flat
3 Acol Road
London NW6 3AA
Understanding major life issues leads to personal growth.

For weekends on Spiritual Growth, Meditation etc. write to:
Dr Singha
The Natural Therapeutic Centre
The Old Rectory
Gislingham
Suffolk

Chapter Three

Books

Regenerative Diet by Dr John R. Christopher
Available from:
Genesis Books
188 Eold Street
London EC1 V9BP
A very thorough, interesting, informative and comprehensive guide to food
values, mineral, vitamin etc content. Also exciting recipes.

Gluten Free Cooking by Rita Greer
A lively interesting attitude to cooking without gluten foods, although *some*
of her inclusions which are non gluten are not really advisable — bacon,
tea, coffee etc. Yet well worth buying. Available from Thorsons.

Wild Food by Roger Phillips (Pan)
A beautifully illustrated (mouthwatering) and very encouraging book on
using common plants, seaweeds etc for tantalising and tasty meals.

Back to Eden Cookbook by Kloss Archives
Very much like his other books, simple, sound and readable. Available from
Genesis Books.

The Complete Raw Juice Therapy by Susan Charmine
A comprehensive guide to healing by using raw juices. There are many
recipes for specific ailments. Available from Thorsons.

Raw Vegetable Juices by Dr N. Walker
A classic work on the subject by this man now 107 years old: on the properties, ways and means of using raw juices in your diet for good health and healing. Available from Genesis Books.

Health Magic Through Chlorphyll by Dr Bernard Jensen
Trapping vital forces, energy and sun to be used enjoyably in our diet. Illustrated. Available from Genesis Books.

Live Foods by George and Doris Fathman
Natural fruit grain and green leaf recipes on bread, pastry, puddings, salads etc. Available from Genesis Books.

Raw Energy by Leslie and Susannah Kenton
An encouraging guide to eating well on energy-giving foods. Available from Thorsons.

Sprout for the Love of Everybody by V. P. Kulvinskas
A nutritional evaluation of sprouts and grasses. Available from Genesis Books.

Water Can Undermine Your Health by Dr N. Walker
Drinking water and its impurities and its disease-causers. Available from Genesis Books.

Hippocrates Live Food Program by Dr Ann Wigmore
A concise guide to healthful eating and living, help on weight loss, youthful rejuvenation and more. Available from Genesis Books.

The Bean and Lentil Cookbook by Pamela Dixon (Thorsons)
Colourful, inexpensive and interesting recipes.

The Unheated Greenhouse by Ronella H. Menage
Making the most of free heat and growing your own food. Available from Thorsons.

A Month by Month Guide to Organic Gardening by Lawrence D. Hills
This well-known organic pioneer gives us an easy to follow book on the subject. Available from Thorsons.

Chinese Cookery by Ken Hom (BBC Publications)
An inspirational book.

Addresses

The College of Dietary Therapy
Hillborough
Ashley
Tiverton
Devon EX16 5PA
Enquiries to:
21a Matyr Road
Guildford
Surrey GU1 4LE
A course available.

Sage Health International
For recipes, advice, food
Contact:
1F, 5 Sedley Place
London W1
Tel: 01 408 1845

CAMHEALTH
Campaign for Healthy Food
For information and help write to:
7 Castle Street
Tonbridge
Kent
Tel: (0732) 304540

For a range of herbal teas (blended) write to:
Jill Davies
Natural Herbal Foods
Thornham Herb Garden
Thornham Magna
Nr Eye
Suffolk
Tel: Mellis 510
Mail order service. Send SAE for brochure.
Also for a complete and detailed book on herbal teas: *A Garden of Miracles*
by Jill Davies, published by Muller, Blond and Briggs.

A New Restaurant Concept — French cuisine naturelle
Elephant and Butterflies
Caterstar Ltd
67 Charlotte Street
London W1
Tel: 01 580 1732
Fine cooking done with pure, natural organic food.

Chapter Four

Books

Doctor-Patient Handbook by Dr B. Jensen
An informative, amusing book on reversal process and healing crisis experienced through elimination and detoxification. Useful reading. Available Genesis Books.

The Anatomy Coloring Books Kapit and Elson
An excellent self-tutor on the body and its parts and workings. Very helpful.

Massage and Meditation by George Downing
A hard to find but really lovely book. Available through:
Holistic Research Company
Bright Haven
Robins Lane
Lolworths
Cambridge CB3 8HA

Iridology by Dorothy Hall
An easily understandable book on the subject. Available through Genesis Books.

Natural Therapeutics by Henry Lindlar
A pioneer in nature cure, these books are basic bookshelf reading.
Volume One   — *Philosophy of Natural Therapeutics*
Volume Two   — *Practice of Natural Therapeutics*
Volume Three — *Dietetics*
Available from the Holistic Research Company.

Addresses

Touch For Health — British Association
For further information ring 0494 37409
Lectures, workshops for a practical guide to natural preventative health care.

Rolfing after Dr Ida Rolf
For more information contact:
Kathleen Webster
2 Neal's Yard
Covent Garden
London WC2
A therapy of touch for massage.

Aromatherapy
An ancient healing method using essential oils of plants massaged into the body. For further information contact:
London School of Aromatherapy
42a Hillfield Park
London N10 3QS

164

British School — Reflex Zone Therapy
25 Brooks Mews
London W1Y 1LF

For all forms of Natural Healing methods — herbalism, iridology, massage etc contact:
Kitty Campion
24a Aubrey House
7 Maida Vale
London W2
Tel: 01 723 3771
Her book, *The Handbook of Herbal Health* (Sphere), is a comprehensive, detailed, modern, lively, sympathetic herbal with advice on many problems and diseases. An excellent choice for a small collection.

Chapter Five

Books

Childhood Diseases by Dr John R. Christopher
A compendium of diseases in easily categorised (alphabetical) order, with definitions, causes, herbal aids and many general natural treatments. It should be in every First Aid cupboard. Available from Genesis Books.

School of Natural Healing by Dr John R. Christopher
A masterly herbal reference work, encyclopedic in scale. Brilliant and a Bible to me. Available from Genesis Books.

A Modern Herbal by Mrs M. Grieve (Penguin)
An excellent companion to Dr Christopher's *School of Natural Healing*. Such research has not been carried out before or since Mrs Grieve's masterpiece. Contains formulas, historical facts, folklore, chemistry analysis etc.

Three Day Cleansing Program and *Rejuvenation through Elimination* by Dr John R. Christopher
Small volumes outlining 'detoxification' — very useful. Available from Genesis Books.

Nature has a Remedy by Dr Jensen
Physical, mental or spiritual — there is an answer — a lovely book well worth reading. Available from Genesis Books.

Health Secrets of Plants and Herbs by Maurice Mességué (Pan)
This worldly herbalist has written down many of his recipes and ideas on using nature to heal — well worth reading.

The Home Herbal by Barbara Griggs (Pan)
A very useful modern book, with complaints listed alphabetically.

The Illustrated Herbal Handbook by Juliette de Bairacli Levy (Faber & Faber)
The wise and now old herbalist produced this wonderful and personal herbal many years ago now but it still makes unusual and informative reading.

The Dictionary of Vitamins by Leonard Mervyn (Thorsons)
The best book on the subject yet, deep, knowledgeable and leaving no question on the subject unanswered.

Minerals by Miriam Polunin
What they are and why we need them. Available from Thorsons.

Hygienia: A Woman's Herbal by Jeannie Parvate
A wonderful book for both men and women — it should be on every bookshelf. Available from Genesis Books.

The Colon Health Handbook by Robert Gray
An excellent and eye-opening account of the most misused area of our body. Important reading. Available from Genesis Books.

Tissue Cleansing Through Bowel by Dr Jensen
A larger version of Robert Gray's book although I'd always advise buying *both*. An excellent book, much shown to my patients. Available from Genesis Books.

The Way of Herbs by Michael Tierra
This book *must* be bought and read, it is wonderful. Among other teachers, Dr Christopher was a great influence. Just read it! Available from Genesis Books.

Handbook of Bach Flower Remedies by Philip Chancellor
An in-depth guide, with case histories and colour paintings of the flowers. Very helpful and beautiful. Available from Genesis Books, or from the Centre, see under Chapter Two above.

Chapter 6

Books

The Beginners Book of Tai Chi Chuan by Seow Poon-Shing
A lovely little introductory yet highly informative book. Available from Genesis Books.

Body Learning
An introduction to the Alexander Technique. An excellent beginners' book. Available from Changes Bookshop.

Yoga for Rejuvenation by Nergis Dalal
The book interprets the universal philosophy of yoga for the beginner. Available from Thorsons.

Reflexology Today by Doreen E. Bayly (Thorsons)
An easy guide to this subject. Available from Genesis Books.

How to Meditate: A Guide to Self-Discovery by Lawrence Le Shan
This book allows you to choose your own meditational path in a helpful way. Available from Thorsons.

Work Out Magazine
A total fitness magazine published by Wellington Video Publications.

Dancercise
For a list of venues and classes on jazz, classical etc dancing:
Tel: 01 560 3300/568 1751
See also *Dancercise Book* by Phyllis Greene Morgan

Alternative Sitting
A range of chairs designed to encourage healthier, more productive sitting.
P. O. Box 42
Abingdon
Oxfordshire OX14 2EH
Tel: (0235) 22777

Birkenstocks Shoes
Footprints
116 Bodian Avenue
Tuffley
Gloucester GL4 0TN
Tel: 0452 21968
Excellent range of light, comfortable, contouring shoes. I wear them myself and they have greatly aided personal foot and spine problems.

Natural Flow
Burwash
East Sussex
Tel: 0435 882 482
For many of the herbal teas and treatments recommended in this chapter.

Addresses

BHMA
The British Herbal Medicine Association
Lane House
Cauling
Keighley
West Yorkshire BD22 0LX

The Herb Society
77 Great Peters Street
London SW1P 2EZ
Tel: 01 222 3634
For information, meetings, quarterly magazine.

167

For weekend introductory courses on herbs and their many uses contact:
Jill Davies
Thornham Herb Garden
Thornham Magna
Nr Eye
Suffolk
Tel: Mellis 510

The School of Natural Healing UK
Co-directors — Kitty Campion and Jill Davies
For details on HD (Herbal Diploma) and MH (Master Herbalist) courses
and a list of qualified practitioners all over the UK contact:
The School of Natural Healing
Thornham Herb Garden
Thornham Magna
Nr Eye
Suffolk
The school was founded over half a century ago in Utah, USA, by Dr
Christopher (their top herbalist). This UK facility enables more people to
learn the art of herbal medicine. Its teachings differ from European ideas
mostly because it is based on many more cultures and has been used for
centuries; it is a major street medicine in the USA now ensuring up-to-date
knowledge. The school specialises in female problems, pre-conception,
pregnancy and babies.

For ½ kilo amounts of most herbs:
Gerard House
736 Christchurch Road
Bournemouth
Dorset BH7 6B2

For a chain of helpful wholefood/healthfood stores contact:
Ray Hill
Healthstores Wholesale Ltd
Queens Road
Nottingham NG2 3AY

For herbs, help and advice over the counter:
Baldwins
173 Walworth Road
London SE17
Tel: 01 703 5550

For fresh herbs and plants:
Hollington Nurseries Ltd
Woolton Hill
Newbury
Berks RG15 9XT

168

British Herb Trade Association
write to:
Geoffrey Lloyd
Hereford Herbs
Rememheem House
Ocley
Pychard
Herefordshire HR1 3RB
For more help, advice and addresses of other herb nurseries. Also herbal gardening courses etc.

For advice on organic gardening:
The Soil Association
Walnut Tree Manor
Haughley
Stowmarket
Suffolk IP14 3RS

Books also available from:
Farida Davidson
Bright Haven
Robins Lane
Lolworth
Cambridge CB3 8HH.

Index

173